Colette and the
Silver Samovar

ORCA
YOUNG
READERS

Colette and the Silver Samovar

NANCY BELGUE

ORCA BOOK PUBLISHERS

Library and Archives Canada Cataloguing in Publication

Belgue, Nancy, 1951-
Colette and the silver samovar / written by Nancy Belgue.
(Orca young readers)

Issued also in an electronic format.
ISBN 978-1-55469-321-4

I. Title. II. Series: Orca young readers
PS8553.E4427C64 2010   jC813'.6   C2010-903530-5

First published in the United States, 2010
Library of Congress Control Number: 2010928825

Summary: Colette's family is torn apart by events and attitudes she cannot control, but she is determined to find a way to mend the rifts that threaten to destroy the people she loves.

Mixed Sources
Product group from well-managed forests,
controlled sources and recycled wood or fiber
www.fsc.org   Cert no. SW-COC-000952
© 1996 Forest Stewardship Council
FSC

Orca Book Publishers is dedicated to preserving the environment and has printed this book on paper certified by the Forest Stewardship Council.

Orca Book Publishers gratefully acknowledges the support for its publishing programs provided by the following agencies: the Government of Canada through the Canada Book Fund and the Canada Council for the Arts, and the Province of British Columbia through the BC Arts Council and the Book Publishing Tax Credit.

Typesetting by Nadja Penaluna
Cover artwork by Simon Ng
Author photo by Max Wedge

ORCA BOOK PUBLISHERS
PO Box 5626, Stn. B
Victoria, BC Canada
V8R 6S4

ORCA BOOK PUBLISHERS
PO Box 468
Custer, WA USA
98240-0468

www.orcabook.com
Printed and bound in Canada.
13 12 11 10 • 4 3 2 1

To Terry

Chapter 1

This morning, when the elevator in my apartment got stuck between the twelfth and the fourteenth floors, right where thirteen should have been, I knew right away that something bad was going to happen.

There were two other people in the elevator with me: Mr. Singh, who lives on the same floor as my family and me, and Auntie Graves, an old lady who reminds me of a little brown mouse. When the elevator bounced to a stop, she started moaning and shivering. Mr. Singh kept telling her that everything was going to be all right. He pressed the red button, and a loud alarm started ringing. This made Auntie Graves sink to the ground and start beating at her chest with her fist.

I plopped right down beside her. "This happens all the time," I said. "My father says this old building is run-down. He says it is just a matter of time before it is condemned." Auntie Graves covered her face with her hands and moaned. Mr. Singh shook his head and shushed me.

"See how we're stuck between twelve and fourteen, right where the thirteenth floor should be? Do you know that the number *thirteen* is unlucky?" I asked.

Auntie Graves began rocking back and forth.

"Some airports don't even have a terminal thirteen," I said. "And some streets don't have a house numbered thirteen. Race-car drivers never choose that number for their cars." I was just warming up, but Mr. Singh grabbed my arm and pulled me up.

"You need to stop talking now," he said. Mr. Singh has serious brown eyes and a snowy turban on his head. He has a gentle voice and always gives me wrapped candies, but today he was looking very stern.

Auntie Graves started gasping for breath.

"She's hyperventilating," I pointed out. That's when people breathe too fast because they are scared. I know all about this because I am going to be a writer, and I once made a character in a story I wrote hyperventilate because she saw a ghost! I even made that character faint!

Mr. Singh knelt down and told Auntie Graves to put her head between her knees and breathe slowly. He was a doctor in Pakistan, but now he works as a janitor.

I watched with interest as she tried this. When I wrote my story, I found out that one of the ways to help someone who is hyperventilating is to give them a paper bag to breathe into, so I opened my backpack and took out my lunch. I dumped it on the elevator floor and gave the paper bag to Auntie Graves. I liked Mr. Singh and didn't want him to be mad at me.

The electricity started humming, and the cables began to move. The elevator started up with a heave-ho. I'd been trapped on a roller coaster once, and it had started in the same way—with a big jerk. When we got to the ground floor, a crowd of people was standing in the lobby. Mr. Singh helped Auntie Graves over to a rickety chair, and she sat down, still clutching my paper bag.

He turned to me and said, "You are lovely child. Talk too much sometimes."

I just like to share information. I don't see anything wrong with that.

My father says that I need to learn discretion. That's a fancy word for knowing when to say something and when to keep your mouth shut.

I find that very hard to do.

There are lots of things I find hard to do. I find it hard not to tell everyone that I am going to be a writer. My father says I shouldn't show off. He thinks I have too much confidence sometimes. He says I should be more modest. Modest is when you pretend you aren't as smart as you are. Or pretend that you aren't proud of something you've done. My mother says modesty is overrated, and it is good to believe in yourself.

I am also very superstitious. My father says that I should not be superstitious. He says modesty is a much better trait to have.

My mother is superstitious too. She was the one who told me that we don't have a thirteenth floor in our apartment building because the number *thirteen* is unlucky. Most people don't know why thirteen is unlucky. Because I'm going to be a writer, I am also very inquisitive. That's when you ask a lot of questions so you can find out what's going on. My father says this is also called being nosy.

Well, anyway, maybe it's because I'm nosy that I asked my teacher why thirteen is unlucky, and she told me that no one really knows. But some people think it's because there were thirteen people at the Last Supper. Then she said some people think it's because twelve is a perfect number, and thirteen is the bad number that comes after it. She told me that people are so superstitious about the number *thirteen* that they don't even have thirteenth floors in apartment buildings. But I already knew that!

My father says we are only going to live in this old building until things get better. But my mother says it doesn't matter where we live as long as we're together. I like where I live because there is always something exciting happening. Our apartment is downtown in a big city called Toronto. My mother didn't come from this part of the city though. I know this because I overheard Luella, who runs the convenience store on the corner, telling Mrs. Singh that my mother came from a place called Rosedale. Then Luella raised her eyebrows, stuck her nose in the air and pretended she was drinking tea, with one little finger crooked. Once my mother took me on the subway to a doctor, and I saw signs for a stop called Rosedale. I asked her if this was where she came from. She looked at me like I was a mind reader, and so I had to tell her what Luella had said. That's when my mother told me that she had grown up there. All I could see from the subway were lots of green trees and some fancy stores. It didn't seem that strange a place to me. My mother also said her mother and father still lived on one of these streets. I asked her why we never saw them if they live so close by. And she told me that they got mad at her when she married my father.

"Why did they get mad?" I asked.

"They didn't like your father, because he was different from them," she said. Her eyes were very sad when she said this.

"What's so different about Dad?" I asked. "Is it because he's stubborn?"

My mother shook her head.

"Did he ever tell them one of his funny stories?" I asked. I love it when my father tells stories. Sometimes they make me think about life, but sometimes they make me laugh so hard I get a stomachache. I bet if he ever told one of those stories to my grandparents, they would like him.

"No, Colette," my mother said. "They only met him once. But there was a big argument, my parents forbade me to marry him, and he stormed out."

She took a deep, shaky breath and looked like she might cry, so I stopped asking questions, even though there was so much more I wanted to know.

One morning a tall, skinny man with a curled-up gray mustache was standing outside our apartment building when I left for school.

"Are you Colette Faizal?" he asked.

My parents taught me early on never to talk to strangers, but this man was so old, I knew I could outrun him if I had to. Besides, he was leaning on a cane.

"Yes," I said.

He looked me over like he was deciding whether or not to buy me. I stared back at him. Staring isn't polite. Lots of people tell me that. But writers need to be observant. This man was very pale, and his skin had brown spots all over it, like giant exploding freckles. He even had exploding freckles on his scalp, which I could see because he was bald. His blue eyes reminded me of someone. And when he spoke, he said his A's exactly like my mother. That's when it hit me. He sounded just like my mother!

I opened my mouth to speak, but he beat me to it. "You don't look like her."

I knew what he meant. He meant I didn't look like my mother.

And this is true. My mother is tall and thin and has hair the color of honey. Her skin is very pale, and her eyes are blue. I am round, have straight dark hair and brown eyes. She is artistic like I am though. She is a painter and art teacher. She tells me that I get my creativity from her and my nosiness from my father. My father was an engineer before he moved to Canada from Iran. Now he drives a taxi.

"You look like him," the old man said. His mouth screwed up when he said it, like he'd just sucked on a lemon. "You look foreign."

"That's rude," I told him. My parents make a big deal out of being polite to everyone, especially old people, but my father tells me to stick up for myself if someone is mean. After all, he says, if you don't stick up for yourself, who will?

"Don't be cheeky, girl," the man said.

He was talking like an actor I saw in an old black-and-white movie once. I didn't like that actor, and I didn't much like the old man. I walked away, and I could feel two hot spots on my back where his eyes were burning into me.

When I got to the corner, I couldn't help myself. I turned around, but he was gone. I wondered if I'd imagined the whole thing.

I have a very active imagination. I think this is a very good thing if you are going to be a writer, but it can be a problem sometimes. I get scared easily, especially if my imagination is working overtime. That's what my father says, anyway. He says there are no ugly things under the bed. (I don't agree. I've seen them.) He says the trees in the park don't talk to me. (But they do. They whisper at me all the time.) He says the things I worry about are silly. My mother says that if they are real to me, they are not silly at all.

I love my mother.

I love my father too. He is a kind man and a good father, but he is a man of numbers and facts. I believe he is imagination-challenged. Sometimes I wonder how my mother and my father ever got together. Then I see them looking at each other, and I think I understand.

That night, when I told my mother that I'd seen the rude old man with the exploding freckles, she raised her eyebrows. "That's my grandfather," she said. Then she sniffed a little and said, "If I could have one wish, I would wish for my family and your father's family to meet each other."

"Why doesn't everyone just come here for a visit?" I asked her.

"It's not that simple," my mother said.

"Why not?" I asked.

"It's just not," she said.

It didn't make any sense to me at all. Grown-ups make things so complicated!

Imagine! I have grandparents and a great-grandfather living just up the street, and until that day, I'd never met any of them. My father's parents live in Iran. He shows me pictures of them, and they are always smiling. I hope they would smile if they met me. Not like that man who looked like he'd just sucked a lemon.

Chapter 2

I'd been so busy daydreaming that when Mr. Singh told me I needed to hurry up, I realized that I was going to be late for school.

Sometimes I'm just walking down the street and, for no reason at all, I pass right by where I'm supposed to be going and have to turn around and run all the way back. My father gets very exasperated with me when I do that and tells me I need to watch where I'm going, otherwise I could get run over. My mother laughs and tells me that she does the same thing sometimes.

It was October, and the trees looked like they were dressed for a party, in gold and red and orange. I cross a park to get to my school, and there is a community garden on one side, full of bright yellow spiky flowers. They were giving off a spicy smell, and I thought I'd pick one for my teacher so she wouldn't be too mad at me for being late, but a big dog that lives near the park chased me.

I am scared of dogs. My mother is scared of dogs too, because she was bitten by one when she was little. My father tells me that she has passed her fear on to me and that I shouldn't be afraid of dogs until I have a good reason to be. Well, if you could see the long yellow teeth and knotted black hair on the dog that lives near the park, you'd know I had all the reasons I needed. I climbed the tree at the edge of the park and looked down at him. He was drooling, I was sure of it. He was thinking about how many meals he'd get out of me, just like the troll in *The Three Billy Goats Gruff*.

"Go away, Spike," I squeaked at him. He growled and stood on his hind legs. He was so big, he almost reached the branch I was sitting on. I squeezed my eyes shut and wished I had a magic leaf blower that was so powerful I could just blow Spike into the next street.

"Spike!" hollered the man who lived in the apartment building beside the park. "Get over here!"

Spike's ears turned toward the man's voice, but he kept his eyes on me.

"SPIKE!" the man yelled again.

Reluctantly, Spike loped off.

By the time I was really, really sure that Spike wasn't coming back and I had walked the rest of the way to school, morning announcements were over and the secretary in the office was finished handing out late slips. I had to wait until she'd come back from walking all the other late kids to their classrooms.

"Colette Faizal," she said. "Late again, I see."

Mrs. Muncie is actually pretty nice, but she doesn't like tardiness. She always says that there may be some things in life we can't control, but being on time isn't one of them.

"Yes, ma'am," I said. Mrs. Muncie likes being called *ma'am*.

"Don't call me *ma'am*, Colette," Mrs. Muncie said. "I know you think I like that, but I don't."

That shocked me. Ever since second grade, I've been calling her *ma'am*.

"*Ma'am* makes me feel old," she said. "Just call me Mrs. Muncie from now on."

Hey, now. Just a minute. She *was* old! I was about to point that out when I stopped and thought. This is what my father means when he tells me to use discretion. I was secretly very pleased that I'd figured that out. I was so pleased that I didn't even notice that Zain was sitting at my desk, beside my best friend Oprah, until I practically sat in her lap.

"Hey!" I shouted. "What are you doing in my seat?"

Ms. MacKenzie, our teacher, looked up from helping Lotus Liu with her math. "Colette," she said. "I had Zain move your things to the front of the class. You missed the move because you were late. Again."

Oprah gave me a sorrowful smile. I smiled back bravely.

"You are much too talkative sitting next to Oprah," Ms. MacKenzie said. She pointed at an empty seat in front of her desk. "I think you might have an easier time paying attention if you sit closer to me."

All the kids were staring at me, so I put on my biggest smile and walked to the front of the room and sat down. That's when I realized the desk was set a couple of feet away from the rest of the aisle. I was marooned!

"Thank you, Colette," Ms. MacKenzie said. "Please take out your English homework and put it on my desk. Then get out your math."

I got out my homework and carefully smoothed out the wrinkles. I'd written about the man with the exploding freckles, and I thought I had done a very good job. When I put it on Ms. MacKenzie's desk, I snuck a look at Oprah. She was gazing at me as if she couldn't believe we were separated. I winked at her, because that's what people do when they are trying to make someone else feel better, but from the look on her face, I guess it didn't work.

My mom usually picks me up after school. She teaches art to street people in a drop-in center near our apartment building, but she always makes sure she finishes in time to walk home with me. Once I overheard my dad telling her that she should get a real job because we could use the money, but she said she wanted to be able to meet me every day after school and walk me home and that no amount of money in the world would make up for her not being able to do that.

Today she was wearing a bright red cape that made her look like a bullfighter. Her blond hair was gathered into a ponytail on top of her head. It pointed straight up like a spear of broccoli, and there was a paintbrush sticking out of it. She was leaning on the fence talking to Zain's grandmother. She waved when she saw me, and her bangles tinkled like a wind chime. The smell of the incense that she burns in her art studio drifted across the air toward me. My father once said that my mother is a feast for the senses, and I agree with him.

"We are going out for tea," she announced. One day after school, we had a picnic. Another day, we went to the park and painted a picture of the sunflowers, and she framed it for me. And once we took the ferry to Toronto Island just for the fun of it.

"It's a perfect day for tea," she continued as she tugged me along the sidewalk. "Smell the smoke in the air? That's the smell of the bonfires that the fairies build to boil their special dyes. The ones they use to paint the leaves gold and crimson."

I looked at her dubiously. *Dubious* means doubtful. I am dubious about lots of things because, after all, my father is an engineer and he tells me that everything must be analyzed. But when my mother talks about things like fairies, I don't want to be dubious. Secretly, I think that nine years, three months and ten days is too old to believe in the fairies and magic that my mother believes in. But when my mother's eyes sparkle with the fun of it all,

I don't care that my father says we shouldn't believe nonsense and that things have to be proven to be real. I want her to go on and on.

"I know!" she said when she saw me looking at her. "When we get home, let's draw a picture of the fairies painting the leaves!"

"What do the fairies make the dyes from?" I asked her.

She flung her cape over her shoulder as she waved at the sky. "From colors wrung from clouds that brush up against the sunset and sunrise," she said. She picked up a rock and pointed at the burgundy and silver glints in the stone. "And from colors distilled from rocks. And from the petals of fallen flowers or the feathers of birds."

"Where do the fairies live?" I asked.

"Ah," she said. "No one knows. But on crisp fall days like this, when we can smell their bonfires, we know they are somewhere nearby."

We turned down a side street. The houses here were bigger and grander but more run-down than the other houses in the neighborhood. Many had been turned into boarding houses, and the fences along the cracked sidewalk were missing slats. A black cat sitting on a stone post watched us as we went by, its tail twitching. My mother's voice dropped to a whisper. "This is a special kind of tearoom," she said.

"What do you mean?" I asked.

"You'll see." She knocked at a bright red door covered with mysterious symbols.

"The signs of the zodiac," Mom said when she saw me looking. I knew what the zodiac was. I'd seen the horoscope book on her bedside table.

"Superstitious hogwash" was what my father said about horoscopes.

The door creaked open. A tiny person stood there. "Hello, Alice," she said to my mother. "Is this your little one?"

Since I was taller than she was, that seemed funny to me. The little woman grinned. She was draped in a long robe that looked like a curtain of moonbeams. As she led us up a set of narrow, creaking stairs into a small round room, she said, "Welcome to my turret." She pulled herself up onto a seat that might have been a baby's high chair and beamed at us. A brass teapot stood in the center of a round table, and two white china cups with saucers were set out in front of two chairs, one of which had a fat cat drowsing on it.

"Sit," the tiny woman commanded. My mother nudged the cat off the chair, and I sat on the other.

The woman poured two cups of black tea. My mother took a sip and nodded at me to do the same. Normally I don't like tea unless it has three spoonfuls of sugar and half a cup of milk in it, but this tea tasted smoky and strangely delicious. The walls of the room were dark blue, and there were paintings of stars everywhere.

"My name is Soraya," said the little woman. "Your mother told me that she named you Colette after a famous French writer because when she looked into your baby eyes, she knew you were a fellow artist."

"I knew you were going to be a writer," my mother told me once. "I could see it in the way you studied the world. It was like you were just waiting to make up stories. I wanted you to have a name that reflected your destiny."

My mother handed her cup to Soraya, who swirled it around three times, then placed it upside down on the saucer. After a few seconds, she turned it right side up and set it down in front of her, making sure that the handle of the teacup faced my mother.

"What's she doing?" I whispered to my mother.

"Reading my tea leaves," she whispered back.

"There're only clumps of wet, brown stuff in there," I said.

"Just wait," my mother answered.

Soraya started humming. I took another sip of my tea.

"Leave a little bit of liquid in your cup, my dear," Soraya said, glancing at me. Then she pursed her lips and started shaking her head.

"What is it, Soraya?" my mother asked.

Soraya took my cup and began to swirl it. "Let's do Colette's first."

She placed my cup upside down, waited and turned it right side up, the handle facing toward me.

Now she glanced back and forth between my mother's cup and mine. She shook her head and started muttering.

I wished my father was there to say that this was all silly superstitious nonsense.

Finally Soraya spoke. "Both of your cups are showing change." She pointed at a clump of glistening leaves on the rim of my mother's cup. The leaves nearest the rim tell us about the future," she said. "They form the shape of a dagger."

It did look like a dagger. It looked like a dagger I'd seen once in a museum, a dagger with a curved blade that was used by an Egyptian prince.

"What does that mean?" my mother asked.

"It means danger," said Soraya, and then she stopped.

"Danger?" my mother persisted.

"You must be careful," Soraya said. "Watch for the unexpected. Be cautious."

"What does mine say?" I asked.

"These leaves are in the shape of an iceberg," she said. "There is danger here also. It could be related to your mother's reading. But," she said, lowering her voice and pointing at another clump of leaves, "here we see an elephant. An elephant is a sign of wisdom and strength. It means you will know how to handle what lies ahead."

"That's enough," my mother said. She put twenty dollars on the table, and Soraya pushed it back toward her.

"I won't take that today," she said. "Bring me one of your drawings the next time you come."

My mother leaned across the table and kissed Soraya on the cheek. She gripped my mother's hand when she stood up.

"And mind how you go," she said.

It was colder, and the leaves shone with a coating of rain. My mother's red cape was like a moving flame in the dark night.

When we got to our building, we entered the elevator in silence. In our apartment, I hung up my jacket, went into my room and pulled out my journal. I knew there was no point in asking whether or not we were going to draw pictures of fairies painting the leaves.

The magic had suddenly gone out of the day.

Chapter 3

After the tea-leaf reading, I was glad when my father came home and surprised us by cooking food that his mother made back in Iran. He made *khoresht-e-fesenjan*, which is chicken in a pomegranate and walnut sauce. It is one of my very favorite things to eat in the world.

"It's a celebration," my father said. "Your mother and I have something to tell you."

"What?" I asked.

"We have made a big decision about our life," my father said. He reached across the table and touched my hand. "I am not happy working as a taxi driver. The dreams I had when I came to Canada have not come true. It is time for me to take action."

I thought of the little lady in the turret telling me that I would know how to handle what lay ahead. Is this what she was talking about?

"Do not look so alarmed, Colette," my father said. "I am simply going to Iran to talk to my family. I will ask them to help us and will only be gone a few weeks. I have put my pride aside. I will do what I have to do."

My mother sniffed. "What is wrong with you both?" he asked. "Did something happen today?"

I wanted to shout, "The fortune-teller says there is danger here. You can't leave us right now!" but my mother caught my eye and shook her head. Strands of hair drifted around her face like feathers dancing on the wind. My father smoothed her hair up toward her ponytail, but it came right back down. My mother put her hand over my father's.

"We'll miss you," she said.

"I wish I could help you," I said.

"You do help me," my father said. "You give my life meaning."

My mother beamed. My father says that when my mother smiles, she could light up the whole city of Toronto.

"Hamid," she said, "I know we talked this through, but are you sure things can't wait? Just for a little while longer?"

My father shook his head and sipped his chai tea. "Sometimes waiting and hoping for the best isn't enough. You know that I have been trying for five years to begin a new career. Now it is time to act. My parents are expecting me, and my ticket is booked. Alice, we agreed on all this."

"When are you going?" I asked him.

"I leave next week," my father said. "I need to make peace with my father. I need to speak to my mother. I would like to become a teacher of mathematics. I have found out that I must go to school for two more years, and I am hoping my parents will lend me the money."

"You're right, Hamid," my mother said. "Of course you must go. You will make such a wonderful teacher."

"Can't we go with you?" I asked. I remembered the photograph of the smiling people and how I thought they looked like they might be happy to meet me.

"I wish that were possible," my father said. "But I have enough money for only one ticket. Since I will not be earning anything while I am gone, the rest of our savings must be used for you and your mother to live on."

My mother gave me a gentle hug. "You must have faith," she told me. "Everything will be all right."

"Your mother and I have some things to discuss," my father said. "Why don't you go to your room? You must have homework, no?"

My father is always telling me to go and do my homework. My mother says education is fine, but experiencing things is good too. My father says education is the most important thing of all.

I closed the door to my room and looked at the posters of Iran I had pinned to my wall. A few years ago, my father had brought them home for me. He said a travel agency was taking all their posters of Iran, Iraq and Afghanistan off their walls and throwing them away.

My mother said that was like throwing away the baby with the bathwater. I laughed when I heard that, because it seemed like no one would ever do something that silly. But my father said that this is exactly what it was like and that sometimes English has very good expressions.

One of the posters showed the dome of a beautiful mosque covered in blue tiles that sparkled in the sunshine. A flock of pigeons was resting on the top, and worked into the blue tiles were other tiles in white, forming a graceful lacy pattern of flowers. My father told me that this was the dome of a famous mosque in Isfahan and that people came to see it from all over the world. The other poster showed a marketplace called a bazaar. This poster showed a smiling man sitting behind giant bags of spices that were the colors of fall leaves. My father said that the spices had names like turmeric, paprika, cumin, black caraway, saffron and sumac. My father has some of these spices in our kitchen, and once he caught me sniffing the cumin jar. He laughed when I told him I was trying to find words to describe the smell. He sniffed at the jar with me and we made a game out of it. Smoky, he said. Musky, I said.

I tried to imagine what it would be like in Iran. The air would be dusty and dry, because there is a lot of desert there. The pigeons on the dome would be cooing, like they were gossiping to each other. The people in the mosque would be quiet, because they'd be praying. A mosque is a church. I think someone would lead them in prayer, and maybe they'd be speaking, but there was so much I didn't know. How could I ever write about it?

My door opened slightly, and my father asked, "What are you doing?"

I rolled onto my back. I pointed at my poster. "Thinking about what it is like where you are going."

He sat beside me. "I grew up near Isfahan, near that mosque. I come from a small family. My older sister is married and has two children. Their names are Mohammed and Fariba."

"How old are they?"

"They are teenagers now. I haven't seen them since I came to Canada eleven years ago."

I sat up and stared into my father's face. "How come you haven't gone to see them?"

"I have been angry," he said.

"Why, Dad?" I asked.

"Because they told me not to come to Canada. I was stubborn and I was young." He smiled. "Well, younger, anyway. I thought I would be able to work in my profession. But when I arrived, I discovered that it is very difficult to become qualified without a lot of money. Then I met your mother and we got married. And then we had you!"

"Did your parents ever meet Mom?" I asked.

He shook his head. "They were angry with me for my stubborn head and for marrying without their blessing. Many things were said between us. These words have stood in the way for ten years, like stones in a wall."

"Do they know about me?" I asked.

"Of course they do," he said.

"Do you think they would like to meet me?"

He reached over and ruffled my hair. "It would be their greatest delight."

Again I wanted to tell my father that the tiny woman in the tearoom had told my mother and me that there was danger coming, but the look on his face stopped me.

"When I was small," my father said, "I had a nursemaid who told me wonderful stories, all about ancient Persia."

"Where's that?" I asked.

"Persia is what Iran used to be called," he said. "It is a very old country, full of history." He hugged me close to him. "Let me tell you one of my nursemaid's favorite stories. It is called *Bahram and the Snake Prince*."

My father hardly ever talked about Iran. My mother once said he tried so hard to be a Canadian that he gave up thinking about where he came from.

"There was a time and there wasn't a time in the long ago," my father began, "when a son named Bahram was born to a cocoon peeler and his wife." My father's voice was deep and rumbly with the hint of foreign places, just like the spices in our cupboard. "But Bahram's father died, and his mother had to raise him alone, and she was very poor. Soon the day came," my father went on, "when Bahram and his mother had one last thing of value to sell, and that was their samovar."

"Just like the one we have," I said.

"Yes," nodded my father. "Very much like that one."

An Iranian friend had given the silver samovar to my father when he'd married my mother. It was our most precious possession, used for brewing tea on only the most special occasions.

"What happened next?" I asked.

30

"Well, Bahram's mother did what she had to do. Although it grieved her to part with it, the samovar was sold for three hundred dirhams."

"Is that a lot of money?" I asked.

"It was a great deal of money. Especially in those days," said my father. "And Bahram was old enough by then for his mother to give him some of the money and tell him to go and buy some cocoons and learn how to make silk the way his father had."

My mother poked her head in the door. When she saw that my father was telling a story, she came and sat on the floor beside the bed. She hugged her knees to her chest and rested her head against my father's leg. "Go on," she said. "I like to hear the stories too."

"So Bahram took a hundred dirhams from his mother and went to the bazaar," continued my father. "While he was looking for cocoons to buy, he saw three men beating a bag with a stick. Bahram went to the men and asked what they were doing. When they told him that there was a cat in the bag, Bahram told them not to beat a poor animal and to let it go. 'Why should we release a worthless cat?' they jeered. 'If your heart bleeds so much for this animal, then give us a hundred dirhams, and we'll let it go.' So Bahram gave the men his money and set the cat free. The cat rubbed against Bahram's leg and said, 'Kindness is always remembered.' Then it walked away."

"What did his mother say?" I asked, thinking of the poor family with nothing to eat.

My father said, "Bahram's mother did not scold him. Instead, the next morning, she said that he had done well, because animals were in the world before people, and we must protect them. Then she gave him another hundred dirhams and sent him to the bazaar to find cocoons to start his business."

"I hope he does it this time," I said.

"On the way to the bazaar, he ran into some children dragging a dog to the top of the town wall to throw him down. 'Don't hurt the animal,' Bahram pleaded. They said, 'If your heart bleeds for this dog, give us a hundred dirhams and he will be yours.' Bahram gave the children his money and untied the dog. The dog placed a paw upon his knee and said, 'Those who have done a good deed will receive good in return.' Then it ran away."

"Oh no," I said. "Soon they won't have any money left!"

"That may be so," my father said. "But again, Bahram's mother did not scold him. Instead, the next morning, she gave him the last of their money and told him that now he must save them from starvation. All day he searched for cocoons to buy, but by evening he was still empty-handed. At the edge of the town, he saw a group of men gathering sticks to build a fire. When the fire was blazing, one man picked up a box and started to add it to the blaze. 'What have you there?' Bahram asked the man. 'It is an animal,' the man replied. 'Why would you want to burn an animal? asked Bahram. And the man laughed and said, 'If your heart bleeds so much for this animal, then give me a hundred dirhams and it will be yours.' And because Bahram could not bear to see an animal harmed, he forgot what his mother had said and gave the man his last hundred dirhams."

"He didn't!" I said, sitting straight up on the bed.

"Sometimes you must do what is right whether or not it is in your best interests," said my mother.

"What was in the box?" I asked, poking my father and reminding him to get back to the story.

"It was a snake," my father said. "Bahram jumped away when he saw it, thinking the snake would spit poison at him. But this was a very special snake. 'Don't fear me,' he said to Bahram. 'You have saved my life. Snakes do not harm those who bring no harm to them. Indeed, we are the guardians of the hearth.'

"Bahram hung his head in his hands. The snake asked why he was sad. 'I have spent my last one hundred dirhams,' Bahram told the snake. 'My mother and I will starve.'"

"Exactly!" I said. "What is he going to do now?"

My mother shook my fingers lightly. "Tell me that you would have done the same thing," she said.

"I couldn't let you starve!" I said.

"But you couldn't let an innocent creature die either, could you?" asked my mother.

"No," I said. But I wasn't sure. I didn't know! "What happened then?" I asked my father.

My father glanced at his watch. "I think I will have to tell you the rest of the story tomorrow," he said. "It's after ten o'clock."

"No!" I said. "I won't be able to sleep unless I know what happens!"

"Tomorrow," my father said. He yawned. "Even I am getting tired. I have to work tomorrow!" He leaned over and kissed my cheek. "Sleep well."

After he left, my mother pulled the covers up to my neck and tucked the edges tightly under the mattress. "That's how it must feel to be in a cocoon," she said.

"Do you think Bahram and his mother starve?" I asked her.

"I don't think so," my mother said. "I like to believe that no good deed goes unnoticed."

"I wish Dad didn't have to go away," I murmured.

"I wish he didn't have to go either, but he does. He needs to do it just as much for himself as for us. Do you understand that?"

"Why can't things stay like they are right now?" I asked. The words of the fortune-teller echoed in my head. *Beware of danger*.

"Nothing stays the same forever," my mother said. "It is just the way life is." She nudged me. "Not all change is bad, you know."

I didn't know about that. In one day, I'd lost my seat beside my best friend and found out my father was going far away. If this was change, who needed it?

"Go to sleep now," my mother whispered. Then she went out and pulled the door shut.

I stared out at the night sky. There were ghosts out there, I thought—lots of ghosts, wandering around looking for places to sleep. My mother tells me that I need to think peaceful thoughts before bed, but sometimes my brain gets clogged up like a kitchen sink. One thought would not drain away. It kept swirling around and around and around.

Beware of danger, beware of danger, beware of danger.

Chapter 4

My father had already gone to work when I got up the next morning. As I poured cereal into my bowl, I wondered how the story of *Bahram and the Snake Prince* would end. As a writer, I saw nothing but trouble ahead.

My mother put on her red cape and started to pack my lunch. Sometimes she does things backward like that. My father says she is eccentric, which means she doesn't do things the way most people do.

On the way to school, my mother hummed a song under her breath. She always hums when she is worried. My feet felt like they were locked into a pair of big lead boots.

School did nothing to cheer me up. Oprah flashed me a smile, but then she started talking to Zain like she'd forgotten all about me. I took my new seat right under the teacher's nose, kept my head down and poured all my thoughts into my journal. Sometimes my journal is my best friend.

It was that way the whole week before my father went away. Each day I got up, ate my breakfast and walked to school alone. I didn't run into any of my friends in the apartment building elevator—not Mr. Singh, or Auntie Graves. My mother was helping at a recreation center on the other side of town and had to go on the streetcar earlier than usual, and my father was either sleeping or working.

I waited all week for my father to finish the story, but it seemed like he'd forgotten all about it.

"He's working lots of extra shifts," my mother explained when I complained to her. "He wants to make as much money as he can before he goes away. Now, don't mope. In one month, everything will be back to normal."

The night before my father went away, I came home from school and my mother was polishing the silver samovar. She picked up a clean cloth and handed it to me. "You can polish the lid."

"Tell me the story of the samovar again," I asked.

She rubbed her cloth over the base. The silver glowed like a soft summer moon. "A very old Iranian man who knew your father as a boy gave it to us on our wedding day."

"Where were you married?" I asked.

"Colette," my mother said, "you have heard this story a hundred times!"

"I know," I said, "but it is my favorite story."

"All right," my mother said. "But first we must have a cup of tea!" She went to the stove and put on the kettle. While the tea brewed, I rubbed and rubbed, thinking that, if only this was a magic samovar, I could make a genie come to life and get three wishes. My mother brought the tea to the table. "I am polishing the samovar to use tonight," she said. "Tomorrow your father is going away, and we must make tonight a celebration."

"Why should we celebrate something that is sad?" I asked.

"It is only sad for today," my mother answered. "In one month he will be back, and it will be the beginning of a new life. We must celebrate his return."

"That seems like bad luck," I said.

"Don't be so negative," Mom said. "When the samovar was given to your father and me, the old man who gave it to us said that we would have a long and happy married life and drink many cups of tea with our large family."

Well, he was wrong about that, I thought. It didn't look like I was ever going to have a brother or a sister. It didn't even look as if I was ever going to know my own grandparents. My mother must have been thinking the same thing, because a cloud of sadness covered her eyes. She stopped polishing for a minute, then shook her head and smiled.

"I have invited a few of our friends from the building to join us after supper," she said. "Go do your homework and then come and help me make some treats for our guests."

I put my backpack on my bed and pulled out my journal. I wrote: *My father leaves tomorrow for Iran. He is going to ask his parents to help him become a teacher.* I stopped and looked up at the posters, then started to write again. *I wish I could go with him, but I need to watch over my mother. Ever since the lady read our tea leaves, I have been thinking he should not go. I don't think my mother wants him to go either. But I can't tell him this. And neither can she.*

I heard the door to our apartment open, then my mother's excited voice calling out, "Hamid!" My father was home.

I stuffed my journal under my pillow. My mother was right. It was wrong to think bad thoughts.

After dinner, my father put on Iranian music. As my mother lit the flame under the samovar and put out a tray of desserts, people began to arrive. There were pastries filled with nuts called *baagh-lava* and my favorite, a sweet made from rosewater, pistachios and saffron called *halva*. Mr. Singh and his wife brought some sweets called *boondi ke laddoo*. Auntie Graves brought bananas fried in butter and covered in brown syrup, which she said was how they ate bananas back in Louisiana, where she had grown up.

I poured endless cups of tea.

"Your parents are very lucky to have so much happiness," said Mr. Singh. He handed me his cup.

I nodded.

"If you and your mother need anything at all while your father is away, you must come to us," he said.

Mr. Singh always made me feel as relaxed as a sleeping cat. It was good to know that he was just down the hall.

By nine o'clock, everyone had put their teacups in the sink and said their goodbyes. I stood between my mother and father at the door and shook our guests' hands as they left.

"Off to bed now," my father said as he closed the door behind Auntie Graves. "We all have an important day tomorrow."

I crawled into bed and waited for my father to come and tell me good night. It wasn't until I was almost asleep that I felt his weight on the side of my bed.

"Sleep well, Colette," he said in his softest voice.

I opened my eyes. He was excited to be going, but he looked tired too. I wanted to ask him to tell me the rest of the story of *Bahram and the Snake Prince*, but he gave a giant yawn, then leaned forward to whisper in my ear.

"I will see you very soon. And while I'm gone, you must be very helpful to your mother."

"Will you tell me the rest of the story of Bahram when you come back?" I asked.

"Of course," he said. "It will be the very first thing I do."

He pulled up the covers and tucked them around me. An airplane flew by my window, and he pointed at it. "I will wave to you from the sky tomorrow," he said.

I hugged him tight around the neck. "I will miss you."

"And I will miss you. But I am carrying many pictures of you with me, so I will have your face to look at all the time. And I will introduce you to my parents."

"Wake me up tomorrow before you go," I told him.

"Yes," he said.

"Promise!"

"I promise."

When he was gone, I turned on my side and stared at my posters. I wanted to fall asleep and dream about the beautiful mosque.

Chapter 5

Rain pattered against my window. The white and blue tiles of the mosque were washed out in the gray light. I pulled on a sweater and went out into the hall. Maybe I would start the tea and surprise my father and mother in bed with a tray.

But when I went into the kitchen, I saw my mother sitting at the table, her sketchbook in front of her.

"Where's Dad?" I asked.

"He has left for the airport," she said. "His friend, Marco, came and picked him up an hour ago."

"Gone?" I said. "*Gone?*"

"Yes. You knew he was leaving this morning."

"He promised to wake me up and say goodbye," I told her.

She held out her arms. "Come here," she said.

I folded my arms over my chest.

"Colette," she said, "he didn't want to wake you. He thought you needed to sleep so you would be able to concentrate this morning in school."

"*School!*" I said. "He promised!"

My mother dropped her hands. "Well, you will just have to forgive him. He changed his mind."

"When I'm a parent, I am never going to make a promise I don't keep. I am never going to change my mind about anything!"

"Sometimes we have to be flexible," my mother said.

"Never!"

"Don't sulk, Colette," my mother said. She beckoned. "Would you like to see the picture I drew?"

I inched toward her. Once she drew a picture of a homeless old person that was so sad, I got tears in my eyes. My mother loves people. If it was up to her, my father says, we would have an apartment full of street people.

She showed me her sketch. It was a picture of my mother, my father and me. There were my dad's handsome brown eyes, his serious expression and the little freckle just below the line beside his mouth that made it look like a question mark. She had drawn herself with her hair falling into her eyes and her red cape swirling out beside her. I was carrying a notebook and looked like I was trying to memorize something. All of us had wings! And paintbrushes! And we were painting the leaves of the big tree that grows beside the community garden in the park.

"You drew us painting the leaves!"

My mother smiled and pulled the drawing out of her sketchbook and gave it to me. "I thought we could use a little magic today."

"You're right," I said, putting the drawing carefully on the chair beside me. "Let's have pancakes. I'll make them!"

The sun was just starting to rise, pale and watery, by the time we sat down to our breakfast. My mother poured me a cup of tea and said, "Let's make a plan for every night while your father is away. This afternoon we'll go to the art gallery and look at the paintings."

"Okay," I said.

My mother waved me off to school. "I'll meet you at the front entrance at three thirty," she said. I ran all the way across the community garden. Spike didn't appear, which seemed like a good omen.

Oprah was talking with Zain. She waved when she saw me. Zain gave me a sour look, but I remembered my father saying the best way to handle someone who was mean was to kill them with kindness, so I told her that she was wearing a cool sweater. The look of shock on her face was worth the effort it took to be nice. At lunch, I turned my marooned seat around and faced toward the class. Everyone laughed, and the lunch monitor started calling me *Teacher*. With the art gallery to look forward to, the day zipped by, and before I could even finish my independent reading, the bell was ringing and it was time to go.

There was no sign of my mother, but that wasn't so unusual. She doesn't pay attention to time all that well. I hung around until most of the kids had gone home. Mrs. Muncie saw me as she was leaving.

"Still here, Colette?" she asked.

"My mother's late," I said. It had started to drizzle, and I shivered.

Mrs. Muncie said, "I go in your direction. How about we walk together?"

"What if my mom comes and wonders where I am?"

"Is there a route that you always take?" Mrs. Muncie asked. "We could go that way, and then if your mom is coming, we'll meet her."

"That sounds all right," I said.

As we crossed the park and headed down the alleyway, the graffiti on the walls seemed even scarier than usual. There were giant dragons and wizards. And knights carrying lances and riding horses with wild eyes. There were dinosaurs and a vampire that looked like it was about to jump out of the wall and grab me.

Sirens wailed in the distance. My mother hates the sound of sirens because they sound ominous. *Ominous* means bad things are about to happen.

When we came out of the alley and headed toward King Street, the flashing lights of an ambulance blinded me. Mrs. Muncie *tsk-tsked* under her breath. I guessed she thought sirens and flashing lights were ominous too.

The sidewalk and the street were clogged with cars and people trying to get around the stopped traffic. As Mrs. Muncie and I crossed to the other side of the street, I looked over my shoulder and saw Auntie Graves. She was wearing a triangle scarf that bobbed up and down as her chin trembled. Tears streamed down her face.

"I know that lady," I said to Mrs. Muncie.

Mrs. Muncie looked toward where I was pointing. She gasped. Her face went gray.

I turned and looked back at the street.

One of the ambulance drivers stood up, and I saw something red spread out on the ground.

"Come with me, Colette," Mrs. Muncie said. She pulled me toward the coffee shop on the corner.

I wrenched my hand away and started running.

"Colette!" Mrs. Muncie screamed. Before anyone could stop me, I was kneeling at my mother's side, staring into her face.

There was a puddle of blood under her head, and her red cape was torn and dirty. The paintbrush that she stuck in her ponytail was broken in two. I picked the pieces up and put them in my pocket.

"Get this kid out of here," yelled one of the ambulance drivers.

A thin brown hand touched my arm. It was Auntie Graves. "It's her mother," she said.

The driver's face changed. "Can you take care of her?" he asked.

Mrs. Muncie appeared beside Auntie Graves. "I'll help," she said.

Someone began to cut my mother's cape, and I started to scream.

Mrs. Muncie pulled me away. I clawed and fought, but she was stronger than I was. I heard Auntie Graves telling the policeman my mother's name and where we lived.

Then they loaded my mother onto a stretcher and drove her away.

Chapter 6

My mother says that sometimes we have to accept things without knowing why they happen. She says that's faith. My father says it is better to take things on faith only if you know the reason why. Then my mother says that isn't the point of faith. My father just nods and says that you have a duty to prepare yourself for life, and faith can't do that.

My mother believes in UFOs. My father doesn't.

All this was whirling around and around inside my head while Mrs. Muncie talked on the kitchen phone to the hospital where they'd taken my mother. She asked Auntie Graves where my father was, and Auntie Graves said that my father had gone away to visit family in Iran. "No," Auntie Graves said, "I don't know how to get in touch with him."

Auntie Graves said that she would go and find Mr. Singh and that maybe he knew how to contact my father. Then Mrs. Muncie called her husband and told him that she would be late for dinner because she was taking care of a student whose mother had been hit by a car. I sat at the table holding the drawing my mother had made for me that morning.

Mrs. Muncie lowered her voice and said, "I don't know how bad it is. She is at the hospital, and they are operating. Very serious, I would say." She looked back over her shoulder at me and gave me a small worried smile.

Auntie Graves brought Mr. and Mrs. Singh into the room. Mr. Singh hugged me, and I started to cry. I cried so hard, Auntie Graves took my mother's drawing out of my hand so my tears wouldn't smudge it.

Mr. Singh said, "Do you know how to get in touch with your father, Colette?"

Mrs. Singh put her arm around me. Mrs. Muncie wiped away a tear.

"No," I said. "Maybe my mother has it written down somewhere." I started sifting though all the papers on her desk, but my hands were shaking so hard, I couldn't hold anything.

Mr. Singh said, "Mrs. Singh can have a look. Is there anything you can tell us about where he was going?"

"It's near the mosque in Isfahan," I said. "That's all I know."

Mr. Singh rubbed a hand across his face.

"When can I go see my mother?" I asked.

Mr. Singh said, "I will call the hospital and see what they say." Then he went to speak to Mrs. Muncie, who told him which hospital to call.

"You can stay with us tonight," said Mrs. Singh.

She went to my room and came back with my pajamas, my toothbrush and a change of clothes. That was when I realized that I might not be coming home for a while.

As if reading my thoughts, Mrs. Muncie told me that she would let the school know I wouldn't be there for a few days.

"The doctor who operated on your mother will call us tonight," Mr. Singh told me when he hung up. "Think as hard as you can, Colette," Mr. Singh said. "Can you remember anything else about where your father went? Do you know the names of your father's parents?"

"I can't remember," I said.

Mr. Singh shook his head. I thought of my mother lying on the pavement with her eyes closed and her skin as white as milk. What if she died? I started to shake, and Mr. Singh had to carry me to his apartment and put me in a chair. Mrs. Singh kept offering me food, but I knew I would never be able to eat again.

At midnight Mrs. Singh put me to bed in her room and stayed beside me, rubbing my back and humming softly. I was so tired from crying and shaking that I finally fell asleep.

A loud ringing woke me. I was dreaming of flying like the pigeons on top of the mosque in my poster. I was talking to all the friendly birds, asking which way I should go to find my father, but they kept saying *go-go* and pecking at the ground. I was so tired from flying that, when I opened my eyes, my arms ached from the effort of flapping them.

For a minute, I didn't know where I was. Then I remembered I was in Mr. and Mrs. Singh's apartment and that my mother was in a hospital.

"She is tired and has finally fallen asleep," I heard Mr. Singh say. "Can't this wait until the morning?"

"Absolutely not!" said an unfamiliar voice. "She should be with her family!"

"Shhh!" said Mrs. Singh. "You'll wake her."

"Just as well," said the strange voice. "I demand you wake her up this instant!"

I crept to the bedroom door and peeked out. A tall man wearing a dark blue raincoat stood in the living room with his back to me. Beside him, a woman with blond hair was speaking to Mr. Singh. "You have no right to delay us another second."

Mr. Singh's wife put her hand to her mouth. Her eyes widened. She had seen me. Mr. Singh peered around the angry woman's shoulder.

"Well," he said. "It looks like you won't have to wait until the morning after all to meet your granddaughter."

The tall couple whirled around. I stepped backward. They looked so upset, I thought they might put a curse on me and I might shrivel up and die.

The blond woman took a step toward me. Her hand clutched a large brown purse. She crossed the room and pushed open the bedroom door.

"Colette?" she said.

The tall man came up behind her. He put a hand on her shoulder.

"Emily," he began.

"Are you Colette?" the woman said.

The tall man stepped around her.

"Colette," he said, "my name is Richard Ridley. I am your grandfather."

I looked from one face to the other. The man's eyes were sad and worried. The woman's mouth was trembling.

"Your mother is our daughter," he said. He reached out and tried to take my hand. I snatched it away from him.

The woman made a choking sound.

Mr. Singh brushed by them both and gripped my shoulders.

"The doctor found your grandparents' names in your mother's wallet," he said softly. "They have just come from the hospital."

Mr. Singh pushed my hair out of my eyes, glanced at the man and continued. "Your mother is in a coma. The doctors don't know how long she'll be in the hospital.

Your grandparents have come here so that they can take you to stay with them."

"No!" I yelled.

"Stop that!" the tall blond woman said.

"Emily," said my grandfather. He sounded like our school principal when he wants to summon a wrong-doer to the office. "Perhaps you'd better wait in the car."

Without another word, the blond woman strode out the door and slammed it after her.

"Are you sure?" asked Mr. Singh. "My wife and I would be happy to care for Colette until her father can return home."

"That will not be necessary," my grandfather said. "She should be with her family at a time like this. Would you pack her things, please?"

Mr. Singh nodded at Mrs. Singh, and she disappeared into the bedroom. I grabbed Mr. Singh by the arm. "No," I whispered. "I can't go with them! I don't even know them! What about my father? He won't know where to find me!"

"These people are your blood relatives, Colette," said Mr. Singh. "They have legal rights. It will only be until your father returns."

Mr. Singh nudged me toward the door, where Mrs. Singh handed me my backpack and gave me a long hug. "Be strong, Colette," she whispered in my ear. "Be strong for your mother."

The man put his hand on my shoulder. I shrugged it off.

Then I put my chin in the air as if I was trumpeting like the elephant the fortune-teller had seen in my teacup. Her words popped into my head. *An elephant is a sign of wisdom and strength. It means you will know how to handle what lies ahead.*

The man opened the door.

"It's time to go," he said.

Mr. Singh handed me a piece of paper with his phone number on it. "Take this," he said. "Call if you need anything at all."

Then the tall man pushed me into the hall and away from the only home I'd ever known.

Chapter 7

When we got into the car, my grandmother turned to me and said, "You can call us Grandmama and Grandpapa." Then she turned around and stared out the front window. Every so often she dabbed her cheek with a linen handkerchief, and Grandpapa reached over and touched her arm.

The streets were a blur of lights, black asphalt and noise. We turned onto the street that I remembered seeing from the subway with my mother. There were carved pumpkins on porches and straw men wearing funny hats. The houses were bigger than any I'd ever seen. Some of them looked like hotels.

We stopped in front of a tall red-brick house. Grandmama got out of the car and went in a side door.

Grandpapa stared after her for a moment, then rested his head on his hands, which were clutching the steering wheel. I thought about running away and taking the subway back to my apartment. I checked on the ten-dollar bill I always had hidden in my back-pack. My father had taught me that: *Never leave home without enough money to make a phone call or take a subway*. Maybe he should have added: *Leave a number where you can be reached* to his list of rules to live by.

I sniffed and ran my hand under my nose. Without turning around, my grandfather passed a white hand-kerchief into the backseat.

"Don't wipe your nose on your sleeve," he said.

The handkerchief had little white initials embroi-dered in the corner. I blew. After a moment, he turned to study me. "My father was right," he said. "You don't look anything like our Alice."

"You don't look like her either," I said. "She looks more like her." I nodded in the direction of the house. A light had come on in the kitchen, and Grandmama stood looking out the window.

"Colette," Grandpapa said. "Why did she name you that?"

"She thought it was a pretty name, I guess." I figured that it wasn't his business that she had looked into my baby eyes and seen that I was going to be a writer.

"Do you like school?" Grandpapa asked.

"Some of it."

"I was like that," he said. "I hated math."

"Me too."

"See," he said, "we do have something in common."

My grandmother rapped on the kitchen window.

"We'd better go," he said. He took my backpack as I stepped out onto the quiet driveway. In my neighborhood there are lots of sounds: cars, people talking, sirens wailing, horns honking. Here, the only noise was the rustling of the leaves.

Grandpapa started up the sidewalk, then stopped and waited until I followed him. My grandmother had disappeared, but there was a glass of milk on the table and a plate of cookies.

"Want something to eat?" Grandpapa asked.

I shook my head. He took the glass of milk and put it in the fridge, slid the cookies into a tin and put the plate in the sink. The kitchen was as big as our whole apartment. Every surface glittered.

"This way," Grandpapa said. He walked through the kitchen and into a large hall, where a staircase curved away into the darkness. He flicked a switch, and a giant light with hundreds of bulbs shaped like tiny candles shone down on us. "Your room's up here."

He led the way up the stairs and past a landing that seemed as big as a basketball court. Here the stairs branched in two directions. There was a tiny sliver of light showing under a door at the top of the stairs on the right-hand side. "That's where your grandmother and I sleep," he said, pointing at the closed door. "You'll be in this wing too."

My grandfather opened a door to a room that was painted red. "This room was your mother's right up until she left home," he said. His voice cracked. "As you can see, she always loved the color red."

He put my backpack on a high bed that had a little stepladder beside it. "There's a bathroom in there," he said, pointing at a closed door opposite the bed. "And here's your closet." He cleared his throat. "Do you have everything you need?"

"When can I go and see my mom?" I asked.

My grandfather ran his fingers through his hair. "I don't know," he said.

"Why not?"

"She's unconscious. She wouldn't know you were there. Maybe you should wait until she wakes up."

"No!" I yelled. "I want to see her!"

"I'll speak to your grandmother," he said.

"No!" I yelled again, looking up into his face to make sure he could tell I was serious. "I want you to promise me now. Promise you'll take me to see her. Tomorrow!"

"You are a determined girl. Just like your mother. That's something all three of you have in common."

"Three of us?"

"Your grandmother, your mother and you." He harrumphed and shook his head. "Try and get some sleep. Before I go, though, I want to tell you that I am glad to know you, Colette. I am saddened it took a tragedy to bring us together, but it is something I have wanted for a long time." He stood up and walked to the door. It clicked shut behind him.

It's only for tonight, I told myself. Tomorrow I'll make them take me to see her. I would scream and yell and kick until they did what I wanted.

Remember the honeybees, my mother's voice said in my ear.

"Mom? Are you there?" I whispered.

The voice came again. *You catch more bees with honey than you do with lemons,* it said. How could I hear my mother's voice? She was lying unconscious in a hospital at the other end of the city. But I was sure I'd heard something, and if I could hear her, maybe my father could too. Maybe he was feeling the same horrible ache in his heart that I felt. I sent him a message. Come home, Dad, I begged. We need you.

Chapter 8

"Time to wake up."

I opened my eyes and saw a strange woman looking down at me. I had fallen asleep on the floor.

My grandmother stepped over me, walked to a closet and opened it. "I hope you found the floor comfortable," she said. Her voice was muffled as she leaned over and yanked out a couple of cardboard boxes. "I saved some of Alice's old things. You're pudgier than she was, but I think some of these bigger items might fit." For a moment her voice trembled.

"I can wear my own clothes," I said.

"You will not wear those scruffy-looking things," she said, pointing at the faded jeans my mother had embroidered with moons and stars. "Not while you're staying in this house," she added.

This time, I heard my father's voice. *Pick your battles, Colette,* it said. It was as if I had developed some kind of antennae.

"You look like a fish," Grandmama said sharply. "Close your mouth." She flapped a sweater and a pair of pants at me. "Here, try these. Breakfast is in ten minutes. You will want to shower and wash your hair before you get dressed."

Her face softened for a minute, and she seemed about to say something else; then she changed her mind. "Don't dawdle," she said. She went out and closed the door.

I stared at the clothes. There was a red-polka-dot sweater with brown lace at the cuffs and a pair of brown corduroy pants. My mother couldn't possibly have worn boring clothes like that, and neither would I! Instead of getting dressed, I went to the window. The backyard sloped away to a giant ravine. Last summer my parents had taken me bicycle riding in the ravine. They had told me that there were ravines that ran all through the city. Climbing along a fence at the back of the yard was a family of raccoons.

A gnome-like woman was bending over a vegetable garden in the yard next door. She reminded me of Auntie Graves. I tried to open the window, but it was locked. I knocked on the pane, but the lady didn't look up. I banged a little harder, and she paused in her digging and cocked her head like a sparrow. Then she moved toward the ravine. A small black dog darted out from behind a tree and trotted after her.

"What on earth is that racket about?" said a voice from behind me. I swung around. My grandmother was standing there. "What are you doing?" she demanded.

"Who's that?" I asked, pointing at the woman.

"That's Miss Ethelberta Jarvis." My grandmother sniffed. "She's got to be eighty-five if she's a day. Getting much too old to live in that big house by herself. Her family wants to put her in a home, but she won't go."

The gnome lady was kneeling down, feeding a gray squirrel out of her hand. The little dog was sniffing the base of a tree. "She makes pets out of all the vermin in that ravine," my grandmother said. "Always feeding the raccoons and the squirrels. Making them more of a nuisance than they already are. And that dog. What a pest he is." She looked down at me. "Now get moving. You need to eat something."

I showered and dressed in my own clothes. She was waiting at the bottom of the stairs, and, when she saw me, her mouth went all tight, but I didn't care. I followed her into the kitchen, where she'd put a boiled egg in an eggcup shaped like a chicken. I hate boiled eggs, but something told me I'd better not say anything.

"Where's Grandpapa?" I asked.

"Whatever would you want to know that for?"

"He promised to take me to see my mother today."

"No, he didn't. He told me what you said, and of course I told him that it would be completely unadvisable. Your mother is unconscious and wouldn't recognize you. You'd just upset yourself."

"I have to see her!" I shouted. "You can't stop me!"

"Well," my grandmother said. "I will be going to the hospital today and will speak to her doctor. If he thinks there is any reason for you to visit your mother while she's in this condition, we'll discuss it. Until then, I think it is best that you stay here."

We stared at each other. She didn't blink.

Finally she said, "I tried everything with your mother. I gave her every advantage, and she threw it all away." She looked out the window, and her lip trembled. "Enough of this! I have things to do. I'm sure you can amuse yourself for a few hours." She thrust a piece of paper at me with two phone numbers on it. "Here is Grandpapa's phone number and the number of my cell phone. You can call if you need to. In the meantime, the television's in the den and there are books in the library. Elena, our housekeeper, will take care of you while I'm at the hospital." She paused and let her hand brush against my hair before pulling it back as if burned. "I'm sure everything will be all right," she murmured. "Grandpapa is doing everything possible to contact your father." She cleared her throat and hurried from the room.

I threw my egg at the wall, where it exploded into a waterfall of yellow scum. Then I put my head on the table and cried until I heard her car back out of the garage. A large woman with black hair in a bun came into the room, took one look at the wall and handed me a damp cloth. I wiped up the egg, and she nodded sympathetically before pulling a vacuum cleaner out of the closet. "Go out and play," she said. "Fresh air make you feel better. Come back in little while and I make pizza for lunch." Then she went into the hall. I sat on the back porch and stared at the house next door.

I decided I would go back to my apartment and make Mr. Singh tell me what hospital my mother was in. Then, if he wouldn't take me, I would go by myself. I was nine years, three months and nineteen days old. I would figure out what to do all by myself!

"Help," said a voice. "Please help me."

I followed a brick path to the back of the yard, where it disappeared into a little house. I'd seen something like it once, and my mother had told me it was called a gazebo. High-pitched barking came from the other side of a stone wall. Spike and his long yellow teeth popped into my head.

I grabbed a fistful of dried ivy and hoisted myself to the top of the stone wall. Where was the dog, and why was he barking?

And who was calling for help?

Chapter 9

The dog saw me. He zoomed between the wall and a spot in the back of the neighbor's yard. Every so often a faint voice called, "Help."

"I'll go get Elena," I said to the dog before he tore off again. As I crawled backward, a stone crumbled away from the wall, my foot slipped and I was hanging by a fistful of ivy with my legs dangling into the wrong yard.

"Help!" I yelled.

"Help," said another, weaker voice.

The black dog was back. Foam billowed out of his mouth, his eyes were wild, and his hot, wet breath dampened my ankle. I tried to pull myself to safety, but the ivy tore farther from the stone and dropped me closer to the dog's open mouth.

The vines snapped. As I fell, I wondered if anyone would miss me. My parents didn't even know where I was. My evil grandmother could bury me, and no one would know where to look. I saw my father wandering the streets calling my name. I heard Oprah crying that she was sorry she'd made friends with Zain. Mr. Singh's voice floated through my head, telling me that this is what happened to girls who talked too much. Auntie Graves rocked and prayed.

THUD!

I hit the ground so hard, I saw exploding balls of light. I thought that if I wasn't dead yet, then the black creature that was hurtling toward me would finish the job.

A soft, wet tongue licked my face. The dog barked, then nudged, then licked, then barked again. It disappeared.

The ground stopped spinning, and I could breathe again. The dog had disappeared, but it was still barking. No one was calling for help anymore.

I walked toward the barking. The farther I went from the house, the steeper the ground got. Pretty soon,

I noticed a ragged path where boot treads mingled with paw prints. I crept toward the lip of the yard and peered down a steep, muddy hill into a tangled mess of branches. Was that where the dog had gone?

As if to answer my question, he appeared again, this time bringing a small, yellow rubber boot. The dog dropped the boot at my feet and looked at me with worried eyes. He kept starting down the ravine and then running back and barking at me.

"Do you want me to come with you?" I asked.

"Help," squeaked the voice.

I don't know why it took me so long to understand that the little gnome lady must have slipped on the mud and fallen into the ravine. Maybe it was because I was so afraid of dogs that I wasn't thinking at all. I peered into the ravine. I could just see a fleck of yellow against the dark earth. The other boot!

I grabbed a root that was growing out of the wall of earth and let myself down the hill. I found a foothold against a rock, then another tree branch.

I reached the yellow boot after what seemed like an hour. The little gnome lady lay on her stomach, her right cheek pressed against the dirt.

"Hello?" I said.

Her eyes flickered open. Slowly they focused on me.

"Why, hello," she said in a faint voice. "Are you a forest sprite?"

"No. I live next door."

"You do? How is it that I've never seen you around?"

"I just moved in."

"Oh," she said. Her eyes closed again.

I wondered if the fall had knocked all the sense right out of her. Again she opened her eyes.

"Well, I seem to be in something of a pickle," she said.

"Are you hurt?" I asked.

"I think I have twisted my ankle," she said. "And I did hit my head rather badly."

"I'll go and get help," I said.

"I'd rather you didn't," she said. She rolled over, lay on her back and faced the sky. "You see," the lady went on, "there are some people who would like to move me into a place called a home. And they might think this little tumble is a good reason to cart me off. But I already have a home, don't you know?"

I nodded. I did know!

"I knew you'd understand. I think I'd prefer to keep my clumsy fall a little secret between you and me. And I do hope you'll help me. You look just like a woodland sprite after all. And sprites are known for their ability to keep secrets." She took a deep breath and pushed herself to a sitting position. "You have been brought to me by the forest fairies to assist me in my hour of need."

I wondered if a bump on the head could make someone go crazy. Then I remembered that my mother was lying unconscious in a hospital.

"Have I made you sad, my dear?" asked the gnome lady. "But of course I have. Just look at that frown!" She held out her hand. "Help me home, and we'll have a nice chat." She hoisted herself up and tested her foot, wincing when she tried to put any weight on it. "Give me your arm, if you will. I just might need a little assistance getting back up that hill. Of course, Amos here will be of great help."

At the sound of his name, the black dog pressed himself against the old lady's shins. "There, there," she cooed. "That's such a good boy. My name is Ethelberta Jarvis, but please call me Ethelberta, my dear," she said to me. "May I ask what name the forest fairies have given you?"

"Colette," I said, staring up the hill and wondering how I was ever going to get her to the top.

"What a wonderful name," she said. "Well"—she extended her arm—"shall we go?"

I don't know how we made it. All I can say is it took a lot of tugging, pushing, grunting and groaning. By the time we climbed up over the edge, I was huffing and puffing like an engine on a freight train.

"That's the hard part done," said Ethelberta. Her face was pale. "Now, if you'll look over there in the grass, I believe you'll find a cane. I dropped it when I took that silly tumble."

I looked where she was pointing and found an old cane lying in the wet grass. Then, with her left hand holding my arm, and her right hand on her cane, she slowly limped toward the house.

We clumped up the steps, followed by Amos. Ethelberta Jarvis pushed open a wooden door and led me inside. I couldn't believe it.

The house was almost empty.

"Where's the furniture?" I blurted out.

"Well, dearie, that's rather a long story," Ethelberta said. She limped over to a doorway and disappeared. I followed her into the dining room. A mattress was set inside a giant cabinet that was built into the wall. It faced a fireplace that was laid with dried sticks and pieces of wood. Ethelberta picked up a package of matches and lit a fire. The kindling crackled in the hearth, throwing a golden light onto the dark wood-paneled room. She sank onto a blanket and some cushions that were spread out in front of the fire.

"I live in this room, my dear," she said. "Isn't it cozy?"

I looked around. There was an old-fashioned kettle hanging from a hook over the fire. A brown teapot and two china mugs sat on a wooden tray. On the mantel were stacked a few plates and some knives and forks. Ethelberta picked up a long piece of wire that looked like a straightened coat hanger and handed it to me. Then she opened a metal tin and took out a muffin.

"Let's toast this muffin, shall we?" She stuck the end of the metal prong through the muffin and held it low to the flame. "If you go and fill that kettle with water," she added, nodding at the kettle dangling from the hook, "we can have some tea. I'm chilled to my bones."

I went into the kitchen, turned on the water, filled the kettle and went back into the dining room. Ethelberta sat propped up on three big cushions with her ankle resting on another smaller one. Amos was curled in a ball on her knee and was watching the toasting muffin with hypnotized eyes. Ethelberta smiled. "Just hang the kettle back on that hook, then swing the arm into the fireplace," she said. I did as she told me and watched as the kettle stopped right over the flame.

"That's right, Sprite. It'll just be a few minutes, and we'll be all set. Since this is a special occasion, I think we should open a pot of jam, don't you?" She pointed at a jar on the mantel. "I made that jam myself from wild blackberries I found growing down in the ravine. Boiled it up right here in this old fireplace, just like the pioneers! In fact, since the electric company and I parted ways last month, I live on what I can find in the ravine." She nodded at the pile of sticks beside the fireplace. "It's amazing how resourceful one can be if one must!" Within minutes, we were camped out in front of the big old fireplace enjoying hot muffins with homemade jam and steaming cups of tea. A little color had returned to Ethelberta's cheeks. "There's nothing like a cup of tea to cure what ails you," she said, smacking her lips. She put her cup down, fed Amos the last of her muffin and turned her full attention on me.

"Now then," she said, "tell me all about you and where you came from."

I looked into the fireplace and tried not to cry.

Ethelberta put her crooked old hand on my arm. "Now, now," she said. "It's quite all right to cry, you know."

So I did. I cried so hard, I thought I'd dry up into a speck of dust and blow away. Then I told Ethelberta the whole story.

She shook her head when I told her about the tea leaves and what the fortune-teller had said. She squeezed my fingers at the part about not knowing where my father was. She poured tea when my throat got parched from talking about my mother and how she believed in fairies just like Ethelberta did. She looked thoughtful when I told her how mean my grandmother was and how she wouldn't take me to see my mother. Before I could stop myself, I told her my plan to run away and how I had been just about to leave when I'd heard her call for help.

Ethelberta looked like she'd seen a ghost. "So that's why I fell down the ravine," she said. "I was wondering why something like that would happen."

"What do you mean?" I asked.

"The forest fairies wanted us to meet, don't you see?" Ethelberta asked. "So I could stop you from running away."

"Why would you want to do that?"

"So you can help your grandmother," Ethelberta Jarvis said.

"Help my grandmother?" I said.

"I knew your mother when she was just a wee child," Ethelberta told me. "She was a celestial sprite, she was. Not a woodland sprite like yourself. She always had her head in the clouds. I spent many hours with your mother." She glanced at the door as if expecting my grandmother to come marching up the walk and barge into the room.

"Your grandmother tried very hard to push your mother into a square box, but she just didn't fit. She had all these interesting ideas, and no matter what your grandmother did, your mother kept on popping out of that box. Unhappily, your grandmother never learned to let Alice be Alice. So when she grew up, she ran away, just like you wanted to do." Ethelberta stopped and tapped her nose with her finger.

"Grandmama is so mean," I said.

"That's not meanness, child," Ethelberta said. "It's scaredness."

"What's she got to be scared of?" I asked.

"Some people are just scared," Ethelberta said. "Scared of what other people might say. Or what they might think. Sometimes they're scared of life, so they keep everything in their lives all buttoned up nice and tight, including how they feel about things. That works for some people, but other people need to wiggle their toes a little."

"I'm sure Grandmama can wiggle her toes," I said.

Ethelberta smiled. "Well, now, I'd sure like to see that."

I wanted to ask Ethelberta what was so special about wiggling your toes, but Amos yawned and Ethelberta yawned right after him.

"Maybe we can talk some more about this tomorrow," Ethelberta said. "And Sprite, I think it might be best if you didn't mention our little tea party to your grandmother. I'd like to have you visit me often. But it might be difficult for you to come and see Amos and me if you tell her about"—she hesitated and then continued—"how I am camping in the dining room."

"Why are you camping in the dining room?" I asked.

"Well, Sprite, this house was built by my grandfather, who was a very rich man. By the time I inherited the place, there wasn't much money left. It's a good thing I know how to stretch a dollar! Despite my best efforts, however, my accounts have been dwindling of late, and I've had to sell a few things so I can pay those pesky bills. Well, as you can see," Ethelberta said, as if reading my mind, "maybe more than a few things! It's a good thing people are hungry for antiques!" She chuckled. "Never mind. I have a hearth. I have Amos to keep me warm, and I have these soft cushions to sit on. And I have a vegetable garden that gives me lots of food, and a few dollars to buy what I can't grow. And now I have a wonderful new neighbor to keep me company!" She clapped her hands as if she'd just been given a birthday present.

The firelight flickered over Amos's black fur, and he yawned again. I realized it had gotten dark. Ethelberta must have been thinking the same thing, because she said, "You should get back to your grandmother's, Sprite. She might be wondering where you are."

"She doesn't care," I said. "I think she hates me. Besides, she's at the hospital."

"Now, now," said Ethelberta. "She does care, but she just can't show it. Give her a day or two, Sprite. I'm sure she'll come around and take you to see your mother."

"But what if she doesn't?" I asked.

Ethelberta stayed silent for a minute while she thought about that. Finally she said, "I have to be honest with you, Sprite. I just don't have the answer to that right now. But you come back tomorrow, and we'll figure it out."

"All right," I said.

"Go out the back way, if you don't mind, Sprite. Just so we can keep our little secret," Ethelberta said.

Grandmama was home. Her car was parked in the driveway. I let myself in the back door, crept down the hall and peeked into the living room. She was staring out the window. A picture in a silver frame lay on her lap. Her cheeks were wet. She jumped when she saw me and dabbed her eyes with a linen handkerchief. "Where have you been? You're filthy!" She stood up and smoothed down her hair. Her face was blotchy and red. Her hand shook. "What are you staring at?" she asked. "Go wash up. You look like a ragamuffin! Go on! Get out of here!"

I whirled and ran up the stairs. I hate her, I thought. I hate her, I hate her, I hate her! Who cares if she wiggles her toes or not!

She hadn't even given me a chance to ask about my mother. I hate her!

Chapter 10

They were arguing. I lay on the landing, my nose between the rails in the banister, and listened.

"Elena told you she was gone most of the day, and you don't know where she was?" asked my grandfather.

"She was outside playing. Don't make such a fuss," said my grandmother.

"Fuss? Emily, the child's world has been turned upside down. I think it's important that we try and understand that," said my grandfather.

"What about our world? Our daughter is lying in a coma. She might never come out of it. She might be a vegetable!"

"Stop it," my grandfather said. "This isn't doing any good. All I'm saying is that perhaps you need to pay a little more attention to her."

"I'm doing the best I can, Richard," my grandmother said. "I don't even know the child!"

"I think she needs to go and see Alice," Grandpapa said. "Did you speak to the doctor about that?"

"No."

"Why not?"

My grandmother's voice broke. "I didn't think of it. All I could do was sit beside my beautiful daughter and pray that she is going to be all right. If only she hadn't married that man!"

"Stop it, Emily. This won't solve anything."

"I don't care! She had everything. We gave her everything. Why did she have to do this to us?"

"Emily. She didn't do anything to us. She just didn't fit into our world."

"What's wrong with our world? What's so wonderful about living in a slum and teaching art to people who can't pay for it?"

"Emily, stop. Please, stop. This isn't how we should be spending our energy."

"I'm sorry, Richard. I try to understand. But the thought that Alice might never come back to us, that we've lost her forever…well, it terrifies me."

"What do you think it does to me?"

"Were you able to track down the husband?"

"Not yet. I went through the apartment and found the flight details, but I couldn't find the name and address of his parents anywhere."

"Weren't there any letters?"

"Not that we could find. And Faizal is such a common name in Iran that it is going to be difficult to locate him."

"What about an address book?"

"Well, you know Alice. She never was very organized. Her address book doesn't have one entry for Iran."

"There must be some way we can find him! What about where he worked? Do they know anything?"

"No. He never spoke of his family to them."

"The consulate?"

"That takes time. I'm looking into it."

"You mean he isn't to be found anywhere?"

"Since they don't have an answering machine, Mrs. Singh has agreed to stay in the apartment as much as she can so that if Colette's father phones, someone might be there to take the call and tell him what has happened."

"I can't believe it! I can't believe he didn't leave an emergency number."

"I'm sure he did, Emily. I'm sure Alice knows where he can be reached. But as you know, we can't ask her!"

My grandmother started to sob. My grandfather's voice dropped to a murmur.

I put my hands over my ears and went back to my bedroom. I had seen a movie once about an underground spring called a geyser. When pressure builds up, the water just explodes, and that's exactly how my sadness was inside me.

When Grandpapa came to the door and told me that dinner was ready, I told him I wasn't hungry.

He sat beside me. I wanted to shout at him to go away, but then he picked up my hand and said, "Just give us a little time. Our hearts. Your grandmother's heart…well, it's broken. She doesn't mean to be harsh. I would really appreciate it if you would come down for dinner," he said, finally. "You need to eat."

"Will you take me to see her?" I demanded.

"If you want," he said slowly. "I will take you to see her tomorrow."

I gripped his fingers. "Promise?"

"Yes."

"Are you going to tell Grandmama?"

"I'll have to," he said.

"She won't like it," I told him.

He hesitated, then said, "No, she won't."

We stared at each other. He was taking my side. I remembered my father saying that a husband and wife should always stick together, and I realized that this was hard for my grandfather. I kissed his cheek. He put his hand over the spot where my kiss had landed.

My grandmother had set the table in a great big dining room. Silver dishes glowed on the table. A golden clock tick-tocked on the sideboard. Grandpapa ate without speaking. My grandmother sipped from a glass of wine and didn't speak. Her rings sparkled in the candlelight. I tried to eat, but the food stuck in my throat.

I waited for Grandpapa to say something about taking me to see my mother, but he went to make some phone calls as soon as he'd finished eating.

My grandmother left her food untouched, just like I did.

"May I be excused?" I asked.

My grandmother glanced at my plate, opened her mouth to say something, but then looked at her own plate and nodded.

I went into the hall. I started pushing open doors and peeking inside. A sign that said *The Wrapping Room* hung on one door. Inside was an entire wall of bins and drawers and rollers holding pretty papers. Jars of pencils, pens and paintbrushes sat on a large table.

The next room was full of the kind of equipment you see in a gym. It even had a sauna. Before long, I found myself on the back porch. I thought of Ethelberta Jarvis sleeping on the floor, and I decided I should peek in her window to make sure she was all right. Mr. Singh once told me that people shouldn't sleep right after a bad blow to the head.

"What are you doing now?"

My grandmother opened the door and motioned for me to come inside. "Haven't you disappeared enough for one day?" she demanded. "You really are the most exasperating child." She glanced at her watch. A look of relief passed over her face. "I think you should go get ready for bed," she said.

As I lay in bed, I thought of my father, far away. I hoped Grandpapa would find him soon and tell him that my mother and I needed him. I crossed my fingers and squeezed my eyes shut. I tried to send him a message.

I'll always know what you are thinking, my mother told me once. *If you are in trouble, I'll know it. I'll feel it right here*—she pointed to her chest—*like an invisible telephone line.*

My father laughed and said, *Alice, you are such a dreamer.*

But when he turned away, she winked at me. *You'll see,* she said.

I hoped my mother was right. And I hoped that wherever my father was, he would feel a vibration that would tickle his mind. Then maybe he'd hear my voice and know the meaning of faith.

Chapter 11

The next morning before my grandmother left for the hospital, she sat me down and said, "Don't go wandering around the streets. I've asked Elena to keep a careful eye on you."

The minute she was gone, I told Elena I was going to go read in my room. She nodded and then took a mop down into the basement. I stuffed my bed to make it look like I was lying under the covers and propped up an open book.

I needed to check on Ethelberta. As I started across the lawn, my grandfather's car pulled into the driveway.

"Where are you going?" he asked.

"Nowhere," I said.

He frowned. "I thought your grandmother asked you to stay inside."

"I'm sorry," I said.

"I came to get you," he continued without really listening. "To take you to see your mother."

My knees got all wobbly. I hadn't believed he'd do it. Now here he was, waiting for me. "Thank you," I whispered.

He opened the car door. "Get in," he said.

My grandfather didn't talk all the way to the hospital. It wasn't until we pulled into the parking garage and he turned off the engine that he looked at me.

"I just hope I am not making a terrible mistake," he said, running his fingers over his face. Then he opened the door, got out of the car and headed toward the elevator.

"You should know that she looks quite different," Grandpapa said when we got off on the fifth floor. "She doesn't respond to voices, and she won't know you're here."

I gulped, and my hands shook.

He touched my shoulder and said, "Ready?"

I nodded.

I don't know what I expected. I think I imagined she would be the same as always, only sleeping. And that when she saw me or heard my voice, she would wake up and smile, and that would be that. I really thought she would know who I was and that she would hug me and tell me that everything was going to be all right.

She was lying in a white bed with bandages around her head. Grandmama was sitting beside her, but she got up and brushed past us when Grandpapa and I entered the room.

I took a step forward. A machine beeped, and my mother lay as still as Snow White after she'd eaten the poisonous apple. Her face seemed lopsided, and there was a cut on her cheek.

"Mom?" I whispered. I reached out and touched her fingers. They twitched.

"I've asked the doctor to meet us here," Grandpapa said.

As if he'd been waiting for his cue, a tall man wearing a white coat opened the door and glided into the room.

"Colette," he said.

I kept staring at the stranger in the bed, hoping to recognize the mother I'd seen two days ago, when she'd said goodbye and told me she'd pick me up to take me to the art gallery.

Grandpapa took my arm and guided me into the hall, where the bright light made me blink. The doctor came out too and bent over so that he was looking right at me. "My name is Doctor Maluk," he said. He had brown eyes and brown skin. His black hair was slicked back from his face, and he had a little white tag on his coat with his name on it. "I am your mother's doctor. Perhaps we can go over here and talk," he said, pointing to a waiting room.

"How old are you, Colette?" asked Dr. Maluk.

"Nine years, three months and twenty days," I said.

He smiled. He had white, even teeth that reminded me of my father's. "That's a very good age," he said. "I loved being nine. But I know that you might not feel that way at the moment."

I nodded.

"Your grandfather tells me you are staying with him and your grandmother right now. How do you like that?

I shrugged.

"It must be strange for you to meet your grand-parents under these circumstances."

"Yes, sir," I said.

"Your grandfather has told me that your grandmother is angry about what has happened to her daughter. She is having a difficult time accepting the situation." He waited for me to speak, but I couldn't think of anything to say. All I knew was my grandmother seemed angrier at me than anyone.

"How are you and your grandmother getting along?"

"All right."

My grandfather stirred in the seat beside me.

"Do you know what happened to your mother?" asked Dr. Maluk.

"She was hit by a car," I said.

"Do you know what a coma is?" said Dr. Maluk.

"Kind of like a sleep," I said.

"That's right. In your mother's case, she is asleep because she has had a brain injury. We are waiting to see how long she will sleep. She might wake up in a few days."

I listened closely.

"And then again, she might stay asleep for a longer time," Dr. Maluk said.

"Will she be all right?" I asked.

Dr. Maluk studied me very carefully. "We don't know, but we hope so."

"Can I come to visit her?"

"Of course you can." Dr. Maluk looked at my grandfather. "It's good for the patients to hear voices and have their family with them. We don't always know how much they hear, but it's usually most helpful. How do you feel about coming to visit, Colette?"

"I want to come every day!" I burst out. Inside, I wasn't so sure. The beeping machines and the strange expressions that flickered across my mother's face were scary.

"Are you sure?" Dr. Maluk asked.

"I think so," I said. Tears sprang to my eyes. "It's just that she looks so different."

"It's okay to have mixed-up feelings," Dr. Maluk said. I liked his quiet voice.

"Why don't you start by coming a couple of times a week and see how that goes?" Dr. Maluk suggested. "We'll take very good care of your mother, and if anything changes, you'll be one of the first people we call. And if you ever want to talk about anything, just tell your grandfather, and he'll bring you to see me."

My grandfather stood up and shook Dr. Maluk's hand. We walked back out into the corridor and along the white hallway toward my mother's room. Grandpapa asked me if I wanted to say goodbye. My grandmother had come back, and she glanced over her shoulder when we came in. My mother flinched as if she was having a bad dream.

Grandpapa said, "I am taking Colette back to the house, Emily."

Grandmama nodded. "There's some stew in the fridge." She got up and came to the door. "Did you talk with the doctor?" Her hair was flattened on one side as if she'd been sleeping with her head pressed against the chair.

"He thinks I should come to see my mother all the time," I blurted out.

"Did he?" Grandmama looked at Grandpapa. "Well, let's see about that." She smoothed down her skirt and turned back to the bed. "Don't stay up late, Colette," she added. "We don't want you to get sick."

Grandpapa was silent until we pulled into the driveway. Then he asked, "Are you hungry?"

"I guess," I said.

The house smelled like cooking, and I followed my grandfather into the kitchen. Elena was dishing out the stew my grandmother had talked about. She put a bowl on the kitchen table.

"Thank you, Elena," Grandpapa said. "It was good of you to stay."

"Happy to do it," she said. "Now eat." She squeezed my shoulder as she put a glass of milk in front of me. "I'll be off now," she said as she hung her apron in the closet.

Grandpapa sat down and stared tiredly at the wall. The giant clock over the stove ticked off the seconds. When I had eaten as much as I could, I asked if I could go to my room. He just nodded.

It was like living in a morgue. A morgue is a place where they take dead bodies. I know about morgues because my father used to tell my mother and me stories at the dinner table about taking people there in his taxi. In downtown Toronto, there are lots of accidents, and people need help going to the hospital or to the morgue. My mother used to tell my father that this was a grisly subject for the dinner table, but my father always said that dying was part of living and we shouldn't be afraid to talk about it. My mother would roll her eyes, and then we'd have another big discussion about the differences between what my father believed and what my mother believed. Tears spilled down my cheeks as I thought of my mother's face twitching in her hospital bedroom.

I decided I would go to visit my mother every day and talk and talk. I would tell her about Ethelberta Jarvis and how I had met Grandpapa and Grandmama. She would think it was funny, and she would want to tell me so many things that she would come back from the strange land she was in and everything would be all right.

I heard voices. Grandmama had come back from the hospital. I crept down the stairs. They had moved into the den. My grandmother was sipping tea from a china cup. She placed it into her saucer and drummed her fingers on the arm of the chair.

"She can't go back there, Richard. I won't have it," she said.

My grandfather stared into the flickering flame in the fireplace. "I think it might be good for Alice, Emily."

"No! I agreed you could take her there today, but that's the end of it. You can't subject our daughter to any more stress."

"Dr. Maluk said it is helpful for coma patients to hear the voices of people they love."

"Our daughter wouldn't want anyone to see her like that!"

"Emily, Emily. Colette is her daughter. She has a right."

"She has no rights! She is a child, and she will do what we tell her. Look what happened to Alice. Did your permissive attitudes help her? No! You were the one who agreed to let her go to art school. You supported her crazy idea of working in that neighborhood where she was exposed to all those street people and foreigners! And then when she married that man, you refused to stop her! You always took her side against me. Now you are doing the same thing with Colette, and I won't stand for it, Richard! I won't stand for it, do you understand me?"

My grandfather ran his hands over his face and stared at the fire.

"So while she's in this house, she will do what I tell her to do, Richard," my grandmother said. She leaned forward and stared at him until he looked away from the fire and into her eyes. "And I say she will not go back to that hospital. I will take care of Alice and make sure that she's getting all the stimulation she needs. I am her mother!"

"All right, Emily," my grandfather said. His voice sounded so tired. "All right. You win."

I backed away from the door. No, no, no! I had to go and visit my mother. But how was I going to get there if my grandfather wouldn't take me? I would find a way. I didn't care what Ethelberta had said about helping my grandmother. My mother needed me, and I would run away if I had to!

Chapter 12

The next morning my grandfather's car was gone, and there was a note on the kitchen table from my grandmother. *I am at the hospital, and will be back by 6:00. Your grandfather had to go to his office this morning. He will be home by this afternoon. Elena will look after you. Do not leave the house.*

Elena was washing dishes. After I read the note, she gave me a giant hug and then poured some cereal into a bowl.

"It will be okay," she said as she patted my back. I sniffed.

"Eat," Elena said. "I go change beds now." She left the room.

The cereal tasted like straw, so I pushed the bowl aside. I started writing in my journal. I wrote about my grandmother and her cold heart and how my grandfather looked like a bent branch that couldn't grow straight anymore. I wrote about Elena's kindness and how Ethelberta was my only friend in my new world. I wrote that I was going to run away so that I could see my mother whenever I wanted.

Writing about Ethelberta made me think I'd better check on her just in case she needed anything before I left. I ran down the stairs, out the back door and across the wall, landing on Ethelberta Jarvis's back porch in what seemed like only two seconds. I let myself into her big empty kitchen. Amos was whimpering, and Ethelberta was trying to soothe him.

"Thank goodness you've come, Sprite," said Ethelberta when she saw me. "Something seems to be wrong with Amos."

"What's happened?" I asked as I knelt beside them.

"I think he's hurt his eye," Ethelberta said. "Maybe he did it when we were in the ravine." She pointed at Amos's right eye, which was swollen shut. "I do remember him pawing at it yesterday," she said.

"Will he be all right?" I asked.

Ethelberta sniffed. "When I was a girl, I had a dog named Sullivan. One day he gouged his eye with a stick. We didn't realize it until it got infected. And Sullivan died," said Ethelberta. Her voice wobbled. "I think Amos needs to go to the vet," she said.

"I'll help you take him," I said.

Ethelberta shook her head. "I can't move," she said. She pointed at her swollen ankle. Amos pawed his eye and whimpered. He wedged himself under the stairs where no one could get at him. "I can't afford a vet for Amos," Ethelberta whispered. "I guess I'll have to call my niece and her husband. Maybe I should stop fooling myself that I can keep living like this." She looked around her almost-empty house.

"What if I take Amos to the vet, and then we can think about how to pay him?" I asked.

"I don't think they'll treat him unless they get paid, Sprite. That seems to be the way it works."

Amos had helped me to not be afraid of dogs. He was gentle and had the softest tongue in the world. He was Ethelberta's only friend, except for me. I knew I couldn't let anything happen to him. I would just have to run away later.

"I have to go," I told Ethelberta. "But I'll be right back, and I will help Amos."

"Where are you going?" Ethelberta said. "I wouldn't want anything to happen to you. You must take care."

"I will," I said. As I ran back across Ethelberta's yard, I remembered the story of Bahram. He had given his last dirham to help an animal. I hoped my mother would understand if I was just a little late today. Then I thought, where would I find the money to pay Amos' doctor?

I looked around my grandparent's house. Inside a cabinet with glass windows, silver serving dishes glowed against the dark wood. I lifted a beautiful silver bowl. Would my grandparents even miss it? It wasn't really stealing if I was taking it to help someone else.

Was it?

Chapter 13

I looked around to see if Elena was anywhere nearby. I heard her vacuum running in another room at the far end of the hall, so I took a deep breath and moved a platter over to fill in the space left by the bowl. Then I ran upstairs to my room, wrapped the bowl in one of the red-and-white-striped towels from my bathroom and stuffed it into my backpack.

Ethelberta had told me that she had sold her furniture to an antique store on Yonge Street, so I knew I only needed to go three blocks. The heavy bowl banged against my back as I trudged through the gloomy streets. Rain pattered on the leaves above my head and, even though it was ten o'clock in the morning, the skies were dark.

When I reached Yonge Street, I spotted a shop with a sign that said Rosedale Antiques. There were beautiful old tea sets on silver trays, old-fashioned paintings framed in golden wood and giant china pots in the window. It seemed like a perfect place to sell the silver bowl. I put my hand out to open the door and stopped.

It wasn't right. Even when I had taken the bowl out of the cabinet, I knew it wasn't right. A lady came out of the shop, gave me a funny look, opened an umbrella and hurried away. A little dog barked, making me jump. I thought of Amos, whimpering under the stairs, his eye swollen shut.

I squeezed my eyes together until bolts of lightening rocketed across my eyelids. What was I going to do? I couldn't steal the bowl. My parents would be sad that I had taken something that wasn't mine.

I had to think of another way. Maybe I could work for the vet to pay for Amos's treatment. My eye caught on something glinting in the window of another shop that sold nothing but tea. In the very center of the window was a silver samovar.

The solution crashed over my head like a roll of thunder. I would sell my parents' samovar. It was old. It was silver. It was valuable.

It was as if I heard my mother laughing with delight. *Good thinking, Colette*, she seemed to say. But first I had to return the silver bowl to my grandparent's cabinet. I ran all the way, snuck in the front door, made sure Elena was nowhere in sight and then slid the bowl into its rightful place. Then, for the second time that day, I headed back toward Yonge Street, grateful that the subway was right at the end of my grandparents' street.

I rummaged in my backpack for my emergency money, then ran for the subway.

"How do I get to the corner of King and Dufferin?" I asked the ticket collector.

"Get off at King Street and take the King Street streetcar west to Dufferin," said the man, pointing at the southbound platform. People jostled closer to the yellow line when the light of the train came down the tunnel. I got a seat by the window and read each subway stop as it whizzed by. I got out at King Street, like the man had told me to do, my stomach churning like a washing machine. There were so many corridors and people rushing along that I didn't know which way to go.

"You lost?" asked a teenager with dreadlocks and a ring in her nose.

"Can you help me find the streetcar?" I asked.

"Sure. Which way do you want to go?"

I couldn't remember what the ticket man had told me. Did I want to go east or west? "To Dufferin Street," I said.

"Follow me," the girl said. She picked up her backpack and her guitar. "It's just up here." She guided me to the streetcar stop and asked me if I'd gotten a transfer.

I shook my head.

"Here." She handed me a piece of paper. "Take mine. I can walk. I'm only going a few blocks."

When the streetcar came, she waited until I got on and then gave the driver the transfer. "She wants to get off at Dufferin Street," she told the driver.

I looked out the window as the streetcar drove away. She was waving.

I watched the streets go by. Things began to look familiar. I had been so worried about Amos and Ethelberta, I'd completely forgotten something very important.

I was going home!

Chapter 14

I took my key out of my backpack and opened the door. Everything looked exactly as it had when I'd left three days ago. Except that three days ago, I'd gone to school knowing that my mother would pick me up and take me to the art gallery. Three days ago, I had never met my grandparents. Three days ago, I hadn't known Ethelberta or Amos existed.

I crossed the living room to where the silver samovar sat in its place of honor on the card table beside the bookshelf. Every two weeks, my father polished it until it gleamed.

The samovar was heavier than I expected. How was I going to get it back to Rosedale on the subway? I opened one closet door after another until my mother's bundle buggy fell from its hook and rolled across the kitchen floor. *Look at me!* it seemed to say. *Here I am! The solution to all your problems.*

I grabbed a blanket from my bed, wrapped it snugly around the samovar and wedged it into the bundle buggy. It just fit! I checked my watch. It was 11:30. If I hurried, I could sell the samovar, take Amos to the vet and still get to the hospital in time to see my mother.

I opened the door to the apartment and peeked out. As much as I would have loved to see Mr. Singh or Auntie Graves, I didn't want to answer any questions about why I was here or what I was doing with a lumpy blanket in a bundle buggy.

When the elevator stopped on the third floor, I held my breath, but an old Chinese lady got on and didn't even look at me. I raced through the lobby, out onto King Street, and pulled the buggy for two whole streetcar stops. I wondered if this was how criminals behaved. I shook that idea out of my head.

The streetcar came sparking down the rails and screeched to a stop. An old man brushed by me, climbed into the car and sat down. I tried to lift the bundle buggy up the stairs, but it stuck.

"Need a hand?" asked a gangly young man with a stringy beard and a black dog. He helped me lift the bundle buggy into the streetcar. "You okay now?" he asked. He had electric blue eyes and dark eyebrows. He looked like he'd be a very good friend to have. I nodded.

I gave my money to the driver and remembered to ask for a transfer. Then I sank into a seat, the bundle buggy grasped tightly in my hands. I watched as, once again, I left my home behind.

Another teenager helped me carry the bundle buggy up the long stairs at the Rosedale stop. When we came up out of the subway, he turned the handle back over to me. "You take care now," he said and went away whistling.

Almost there.

My hands shook so hard I could hardly open the door to the antiques store. A man with gray hair in a side fringe and none on top looked up from reading a newspaper. His glasses were perched on the end of his nose.

"Well, hello," he said. "What have we here?"

I pulled the bundle buggy through the store. The man took off his glasses and let them hang from a cord around his neck. He came out from behind the counter, and I took the samovar out of the bundle buggy and removed the blanket.

"Where did you get this?" asked the man. He knelt down and ran his fingers over the handles and along the sides. "I've never seen one this beautiful."

"I need to sell it," I said.

The man stood up, rubbed his nose, then motioned for me to follow him. We went to the back of the shop, where a brightly colored parrot twittered in a cage.

"Watch out!" screeched the bird. I jumped.

"Don't mind Nathaniel," said the man. "Silly bird loves to frighten people." He plugged in a kettle and pulled up a chair with a threadbare, flowery cushion on it. "Make yourself comfortable," he said. "I never like to do business on an empty stomach." He put out a plate of chocolate-covered biscuits and made two mugs of steaming tea. I knew I wasn't supposed to take anything from strangers, so I said, "No, thank you."

"Are you sure?" the man asked. "You look awfully hungry."

"It's okay," I said. I hoped he couldn't hear the noises my stomach was making.

Behind him was a photograph of a woman with four children. He saw me looking, and said, "That's my daughter and her four children. Sylvia, the youngest, is just about your age."

Sylvia had dark skin and big brown eyes, but this man's daughter was as blond as my mother.

"Sylvia is from Africa," the man said. "My daughter adopted her." He studied me. "You must need money very badly to want to sell such a beautiful piece," he said finally.

I nodded.

"Do your parents know you want to sell the samovar?" he asked.

I shook my head. The bird rustled in his cage and shook out his feathers.

"My name is Mr. Murray," the man said. "What is your name?"

"Colette," I said. "Colette Faizal."

"Well, Colette," Mr. Murray said, holding out his hand. "It's very nice to meet you."

"But I know they wouldn't mind if I sold it," I blurted out, hoping that I was right.

"I'm sure you have a good reason," Mr. Murray said. "Do you think you could tell me what it is?"

I couldn't see any harm in that. "A dog I know is very sick," I said. "He needs to go to the vet, but the person who owns him hasn't got any money."

"My, my, that is sad," Mr. Murray said. He thought for a moment. "You know, I'd be happy to lend you some money for the vet. You keep this beautiful samovar. I'm sure you will find a way to pay me back."

I stared at him in shock. A complete stranger was going to give me money?

"But there is something I would need to know, if I'm going to lend you some money, my dear," he said. "Where do you live?"

That stumped me. If I gave my old address, he might try and find my parents, and I couldn't explain to him about all that. So I told him I lived with my grandmother at 121 Maple Street.

"Why, that house is right next door to a house where an old friend of mine used to live," said Mr. Murray. "Her name was Ethelberta Jarvis."

I sat up with a start.

"Something wrong?" asked Mr. Murray.

I shook my head. The bird screeched, "Ethelberta! Ethelberta! Ethelberta! Ha, ha, ha!"

116

"Ethelberta and I went to school together." Mr. Murray chuckled. "I used to tease her something fierce, and she always played tricks on me. One day she put a firecracker in a metal wastepaper basket and set it off right beside my desk. My, oh, my, but did I jump! And our teacher? Old Miss McMullan almost fainted. Ethelberta certainly caught it that day. She was made to write lines on the chalkboard for an entire week. I still remember what she had to write. *I will not play with fire.* I'll tell you a secret," Mr. Murray said, leaning forward. "I had a schoolboy crush on Miss Ethelberta back then." His eyes lost focus and he stared into the air above my head as if he was watching a movie screen. "I'll never forget how pretty she was." He shook his head and brought his eyes back to me. "I've spent almost my whole life in Australia. I moved back to Canada six months ago to be closer to my daughter. Being in my old neighborhood has made me think about Ethelberta from time to time. It's a shame we lost touch with each other. I always wondered what happened to her."

Words caught in my throat like dry dusty cracker crumbs. If I told Mr. Murray where she was, then he would want to go and see her. If he did that,

Ethelberta's secret would be out. Then they would come and take her away to a home.

Mr. Murray looked at me curiously. For the second time that day, I wished someone would tell me what to do.

Chapter 15

We know the truth, not only by reason, but also by the heart, said that pesky voice inside my head. My mother's face swam before my eyes. *By the heart,* she whispered again.

"Ethelberta Jarvis needs help," I said. My hand flew to my mouth. Had I said that?

"What do you mean?" asked Mr. Murray.

"Amos—the dog that needs help—belongs to Ethelberta Jarvis."

Understanding broke over Mr. Murray's face. He shook his head and muttered again about how old friends should never lose touch with each other.

"You can't tell anyone," I blurted out.

Mr. Murray stopped talking to himself. "Are there other things that you haven't told me?" he asked.

"No." Not even Mr. Murray needed to know about the empty rooms, Ethelberta's fall or her twisted ankle.

Mr. Murray drummed his fingers on the table. "I can see you don't want to say more," he said. "You are a good friend, I think." He stood up and walked over to the cash register, punched a button and grabbed the drawer as it popped open. He reached in and counted out some money, put it in an envelope and walked back to me. "Let's leave the samovar here, and we will conclude our business later, shall we? Right now, I would like to come with you to help Ethelberta," he said. "Do you think she would mind?"

"Ethelberta, ha!" squawked Nathaniel.

"I could give you this money, but I think maybe Ethelberta and I should meet again," Mr. Murray said. He blushed a little.

Nathaniel whistled.

"All right," I said. I hoped this was the truth my heart was supposed to know. Mr. Murray put on an old tweed overcoat, flipped the shop sign from *Open* to *Closed* and locked the door. He took me by the hand as we crossed Yonge Street and didn't let go until we were standing together on Ethelberta's old back porch.

He smoothed his side-fringe hair with shaking fingers. He removed a snowy white handkerchief from the inside pocket of his overcoat and blew his nose.

I opened the door and called out, "Ethelberta?"

Her voice floated back from the dining room. "Is that you, Sprite?"

I led Mr. Murray through the dark kitchen into the dining room. As we got closer, Amos's whimpering grew louder. At the door of the dining room, Mr. Murray stopped. I could see him looking at the empty rooms.

Ethelberta raised her hand to wave hello, but when she saw Mr. Murray, her hand dropped to her throat and her voice died away. She closed her eyes.

"Sprite, what have you done?" she whispered.

Mr. Murray covered the distance between him and Ethelberta in five steps. "Are you injured, Ethelberta?" he asked as he knelt before her like a knight in a storybook.

Ethelberta opened her eyes. "Christopher? Is it really you?" she asked.

They gazed into each other's eyes forever, it seemed to me. It was Amos's whimpering that brought them back to reality.

"My wonderful friend Amos needs medical attention, Christopher. I have no idea how Sprite found you, but perhaps this is the way things are meant to be."

"Colette came to my shop to sell her beautiful samovar," he told her. "In the course of our transaction, it came out that she was trying to help her dear friend, Ethelberta Jarvis. I didn't realize you were still living here, Ethelberta," he said. "When I knew you might need some assistance…well, I had to come."

I had crawled to where Amos was wedged under the stairs. "His eye is all gooey," I said. "I think we'd better hurry!"

Luckily Amos was a small dog, so Mr. Murray just wrapped him in a blanket and carried him down the street. Ethelberta tried to stand, but couldn't support herself on her sprained ankle.

"Don't worry," I told her. "I'll go with them."

"I hope Amos will be all right," Ethelberta said.

I reached over and daubed at her tears with the hem of my sleeve, just like my mother always did to me. "He will be," I said. Then I ran after Mr. Murray and Amos.

I followed them into a veterinarian's office about a block from Mr. Murray's store. Mr. Murray was already talking to a woman with gray hair that frizzed out from her head like a dandelion. "This is Dr. Malachi," Mr. Murray said. "We are very fortunate to have arrived before she closes for the day."

Dr. Malachi took Amos from Mr. Murray's arms, and we followed her into an examination room. I stroked Amos's head while Dr. Malachi opened his eyelid and looked at his eye with a little flashlight. She took a needle from a cabinet and gave Amos two shots in the scruff of his neck. As she worked, she explained what she was doing.

"He has an infection in his eye," she said. "It is a very good thing you brought him in when you did. There is a scratch on his cornea that has become inflamed. I have given him a shot of penicillin to clear up the infection, and now I am going to clean the scratch with a disinfectant. The second shot was to relax Amos so he won't wiggle when I swab his eye."

Amos had gone slack and was sleeping deeply on the table. "Why don't you two go out to the waiting room? I won't be long."

"Perhaps you can tell me your story," Mr. Murray said as we sat down.

I glanced at the clock. It was 5:00 PM.

My mother! I jumped to my feet. I had to get to the hospital. What if she woke up and I wasn't there?

"Colette," said Mr. Murray. "Is something wrong?" Without answering, I ran for the door.

"Colette!" Mr. Murray shouted. "Come back!"

For the second time that day, I ran down the subway steps. A different ticket collector told me that the hospital was the Queen Street stop. At Queen Street, I asked a lady which way to go, and she pointed, saying that the hospital was a few blocks away. My chest burned as I arrived in the hospital reception area. A woman was working at her desk and didn't even look up as I went by. I tried to remember how to get to my mother's room, but it was like the corn maze I'd gone to last fall. A man pushing a bucket and swinging a mop came down the corridor toward me.

"Help you?" he asked.

I told him my mother's room number, and he said, "You got yourself all turned around, little girl. You need to go that way." He pointed at another long corridor. "Hey, now," he said when he saw my face. "How about I show you?"

He led me toward a staircase and up one floor. Then we went over a little bridge into another side of the hospital. Underneath us, I could see a coffee cart and an atrium filled with plants and people reading magazines. Some of the people were in wheelchairs. "That's one of the visiting areas," the man said. He punched an elevator button, and when the elevator arrived, he said, "Just go to the fifth floor and turn left. You got into the South Wing instead of the North, that's all."

"Thank you."

"No problem."

It was quiet on the fifth floor. No one was at the nurses' station. My mother's room was dark, but she was there, alone, twitching and grimacing in her sleep. I pulled a chair as close to the bed as I could. I took her hand, put my face on the side of the bed and without another thought, fell into a deep sleep.

Chapter 16

"Colette," said a familiar voice.

I thought I was dreaming. In the dream, the first person I saw was my grandfather. My grandmother was standing beside him, her hand covering her mouth. A nurse in a white uniform stood beside my mother's bed. She looked like an angel, and for a minute I thought we were all in heaven.

Someone touched my shoulder. This was no dream, I realized. I turned to see who it was. It couldn't be!

My father gathered me into his arms and hugged me tight as I started to cry.

"It's all right," he said. "It's all right. I came as soon as Mr. Singh told me what had happened."

"How did he find you?" I sobbed.

"After I arrived at my parents' home, I telephoned to tell you I had landed safely. I thought it was strange that I didn't get an answer, but I didn't worry too much because Iran is eight and half hours ahead of Toronto. But when another day went by, then another, I called Mr. Singh. It wasn't until Thursday evening that I found out what had happened. As soon as I could, I got on a plane and flew right back. I arrived an hour ago, and your grandfather picked me up at airport. That was when he told me that Elena was the last person to see you, and that had been at breakfast! Your grandmother has been looking everywhere for you. No one could find you to tell you that I was on my way home! Where were you?"

I explained about Ethelberta, Amos, Mr. Murray and the samovar. My father just shook his head. "You must never run away like that again, Colette."

The door to the room opened, and Ethelberta Jarvis and Christopher Murray stood there, mouths open. "Thank heavens!" said Ethelberta. She hobbled toward the bed. "My goodness, but you gave Christopher and me a fright. As soon as he told me that you'd run away, I knew you must have come here." She sank into a chair by the bed. "You are a most determined child!"

"I tried all day to find you," my grandmother said softly. "I wanted to tell you your father was coming. However did you find your way here all by yourself? When I think of you running around the streets all alone..." Her voice trailed off. "Thank heavens you are all right!"

I hiccuped. My mother twitched in her strange sleep.

My father gripped my hand, and his eyes were very sad and dark. He put his arms around me and held me tight. "The most important thing is that you are safe," he mumbled into my hair, and his voice trembled. I rubbed my nose on his jacket.

"Is Mom going to be all right?" I asked. I knew my father would tell me the truth. He was a man of science.

A shiver ran through him. "I don't know," he said finally.

I patted his hand. "I think she will," I said. "We must have faith. That's what Mom would want."

"I want to believe," he said. He tried to smile. "I am just so glad to have found you!"

"What did your parents say?" I asked him.

"At first they did not think that going back to school was the right thing for me to do. They wanted us to move to Iran, where I could work as an engineer without further education." A machine beeped, and my grandmother put her hand on my mother's forehead as if she was feeling for a fever. My father touched my mother's hand. "But I told them my life was here with my family, and they agreed to give me the help I need."

"That's good, isn't it?" I asked.

"Yes," he said. "But when I heard about what had happened to your mother, I could not think of anything else."

"Don't worry," I told him. "We'll work it out."

"Maybe so," my father said. "My mother and father are planning to come for a visit as soon as they can get visas," he added. "They realized that too much time had passed without coming to visit us."

"That's good news, Dad," I said. "It's what Mom always said she wanted more than anything."

My grandmother gasped.

"What is it?" said my grandfather.

"Alice?" my grandmother said. Her voice was a squeak.

We all turned to look at my mother. For the first time in days, her eyes were open, and she was staring right at me.

"Sometimes it happens like that," Dr. Maluk said. My father, my grandparents and I were standing outside my mother's room. "Sometimes people just wake up, and we don't know why." He paused. "In the case of your mother, I rather think it was having all of you together."

"Oh, come now," said my grandmother. "That's hardly scientific."

"Perhaps there is more to the story than science," my father said.

I stared at him. I couldn't believe my ears.

"I don't care why she woke up," my grandfather said. "I'm just so glad she is back with us."

My grandmother reached over and took his hand.

My father put his arm around my shoulder. We all looked at each other. My grandmother gave me a weak smile. I smiled back.

"Alice will have to stay with us for a while longer," the doctor continued. "We'll need to run some tests and assess her condition thoroughly before we can talk about what will happen next."

My father, grandmother and grandfather started to ask hundreds of questions. I went over to where Ethelberta and Mr. Murray were sitting.

"How's Amos?" I asked.

"Amos is going to be just fine," Mr. Murray said. "He and Ethelberta are going to come and stay at my house while they recuperate." He beamed at Ethelberta. "Besides, we have seventy years of conversation to catch up on!"

"I hope we won't be any trouble," said Ethelberta.

"Nonsense!" said Mr. Murray. "What are friends for?"

"What do the doctors have to say about your mother?" asked Mr. Murray.

"They don't know yet," I told him. But I knew. It didn't matter what the doctors thought. I knew that she had willed us to come together. I could feel her love wrapped around us like a big red blanket.

Ethelberta could tell what I was thinking. She just smiled and nodded.

And I smiled back.

Chapter 17

The party was in full swing.

Two months after she woke up, my mother finally came home. Now she was sitting in the living room in front of the fireplace at her parents' house. Mr. and Mrs. Singh, Auntie Graves, and Mamanaie and Babaie, my grandmother and grandfather from Iran, were there. So were my mother's parents and my great-grand-father with the exploding freckles. Ethelberta held Amos on her knee as Mr. Murray sang an old Scottish tune. My father's parents talked quietly to Mr. Singh.

After I passed around a tray of food, I asked my father to come outside with me.

But first I kissed my mother's cheek. "We'll be right back," I told her. She nodded. She still had trouble speaking, but the doctors said that if she practiced, she was going to talk and walk just like she did before. Before we left, I went over to my grandparents from Iran and told Mamanaie how pretty she looked in her golden shawl. She patted my head, and her bracelets jangled. Then she smiled.

"You very pretty too," she said.

I tugged my father's hand, leading him down the path to the gazebo at the very edge of the ravine. The darkness came earlier every day. Soon it would be Christmas.

"What is it, Colette?" Dad asked as we huddled together. "Why did you want to come out here?"

Across the yard, we could see the brightly lit windows—little golden squares, like many pictures.

There was Ethelberta, tapping her foot in time with the music.

There was Grandmama, polishing a delicate china teacup before pouring tea from the glowing silver samovar that Mr. Murray had returned to my father.

There was Grandpapa talking to my great-grandfather.

There were my father's parents, sitting together, holding hands and smiling tentatively at all the commotion and trying to understand the English conversation.

But most special of all, there was my mother, sitting in a halo of light, smiling at everyone. I cleared my throat. It was so hard to believe that my whole family was in the same room.

"There is something I've been wondering about ever since you went away," I said.

"What's that?" my father asked.

"I want to know the end of the story. The story of *Bahram and the Snake Prince*."

"You mean the story I was telling two months ago?"

I nodded. "Did Bahram and his mother starve?"

"Well," said my father, "where did I leave off?"

"Bahram had just spent his last hundred dirhams to save the snake," I reminded him.

"Oh, yes," my father said. "I hope I can remember what happens next."

"Dad!" I said.

He laughed. "Oh, now I remember. It turned out that the snake did not want Bahram to suffer for his kindness, and so he sent Bahram to see his father, the King of Snakes. The snake told Bahram to ask his father for a great emerald ring on which is carved a magic sign of Suleiman, the great King of Kings."

"Wow!" I said.

"Exactly," my father replied. "Bahram did what the snake told him to do, and the King of Snakes gave him the ring of Suleiman, but he warned him that the ring must only be given to a person with a clean heart, because if an unworthy person held the ring, Ahriman, the Lord of Evil would enter his heart and turn the world upside down."

Inside the brightly lit dining room, Mr. Murray and Ethelberta burst into happy laughter. I turned my eyes back to my father.

"Bahram was nervous, but he knew his heart was pure, so he accepted the ring. Only then did Bahram learn of the ring's powers. The Snake Prince took him aside and told him that if the owner of the ring was to rub the emerald, a giant slave would appear and grant any wish."

"I hope Bahram uses the ring wisely!" I said, shivering.

"Perhaps we should go inside," said my father.

"No!" I cried. "Please, Dad, finish the story."

"The first thing Bahram asked for was food," my father said. "And then he told his mother that he was going to ask the slave for a giant castle to replace their mud hut."

"Oh," I said. I imagined a shining castle rising high into the sky.

"But his mother wanted to stay in the hut, where she had so many memories," my father said.

I understood that. I would hate to leave our apartment, where the night sounds kept me company and where my slice of the sky was like a new picture every time I went to bed.

"So Bahram wished for a castle to rise up right next door to his mother's hut," said my father. "As time went by, he gained everything he ever wanted: fine horses, fine clothes and even a beautiful princess for a wife."

"What happened next?" I asked. I saw trouble ahead. I always figure out how a story ends before it does. My mother tells me to let myself be surprised, but I can't help it. I think it's the writer in me.

"Another prince who had wanted to marry the princess was angry that a lowly cocoon peeler's son had won her hand. So he sent an evil woman to spy on Bahram and his wife."

I knew it! I am never wrong. I knew something bad was going to happen.

"And so it was," continued my father, "that the evil woman tricked the princess into revealing that Bahram's wealth came from the ring of Suleiman. And, a few days later, the old woman took the ring from its hiding place and gave it to the jealous prince."

I shook my head. The princess should have known better.

"As soon as the jealous prince put the ring on his finger, he wished for the cocoon peeler's son to lose everything, and in the blink of an eye nothing remained of Bahram's wealth. The jealous prince even claimed the princess as his bride. Bahram's heart was broken, but his mother said, 'What the wind gives, the wind takes away.' Then she gave him a handful of dirhams and told him to go to town and buy some cocoons."

"Is that how the story ends?" I asked. "Just like it began?"

My father laughed. "Not quite," he said. "Bahram did his mother's bidding, but got to town too late to buy cocoons, as the sun had already set. He sat down to rest, and while he was leaning against the town wall, the cat, the dog and the snake whom he had saved came to him and asked why he was so sad. He told them how the ring had been taken from him and how he had lost his beloved wife and all his possessions."

"I hope they help him," I said.

"Well," said my father, "that's exactly what happened. The Snake Prince said to the cat and the dog that Bahram had saved their lives when they were helpless and that now they must help him in return. And the cat agreed. She said, 'I shall do it, for kindness is always remembered.' And the dog said, 'I shall do it also. For good must be met with good.'"

I leaned closer to my father. He stroked my cheek with his finger. "Sometimes these old tales teach us many truths about life, do you not think so?" I looked at Ethelberta and Mr. Murray. They were dancing now, an old-fashioned waltz. My mother's face shone like a beacon, and Grandmama was holding Grandpapa's hand. My grandparents from Iran sipped tea while they smiled at the dancers. Grandmama had even asked me to teach her how to say *Welcome* in Farsi, the language of Iran.

In the dark night, I nodded.

My father followed my gaze and spoke softly. "Yes. I see it too. It is some kind of miracle, I think."

"Finish the story, Dad."

"Yes. Yes. So, the cat and the dog snuck into the palace of the jealous prince and found the ring and returned it to Bahram. After he had reclaimed his wife, he threw the ring deep into the ocean, where it remains to this day."

"He threw away the ring?" I asked.

"Yes," answered my father.

"But why?"

"Because he had true happiness. He knew that family was the most important thing of all, and he realized that something so powerful as the ring should never fall into the wrong hands, the hands of those who would turn the world upside down."

I sniffed a little. I always hate it when a story comes to an end. I think it is because I am going to be a writer. And writers hate to see stories end.

"Come now," my father said. He pointed at the window. "Your mother is beckoning to us to join the family."

Sure enough. My grandfather from Iran had wheeled my mother's chair to the window. She was looking out into the night trying to see us, but somehow looking right into our eyes. I imagined her saying to my grandfather, "Isn't it funny how things turn out?"

I squeezed my dad's hand and said, "You're right. The family is waiting."

He smiled and shook his head as if he was still trying to figure out how it was that all of us were together at last.

One day, I thought, when I write it all down, I'll explain it to him.

Acknowledgments

Bahram and the Snake Prince is an ancient Persian folktale, retold many times. I wish to acknowledge the book *Persian Folk and Fairy Tales* retold by Anne Sinclair Mehdevi as a wonderful source of ancient wisdom and a great help in my research into Persian culture. I also want to thank my agent, Hilary McMahon, for her comments and current wisdom. And special thanks to my editor, Sarah Harvey, who was always thoughtful and insightful with her editorial pencil.

Nancy Belgue is the author of many books for young people, including *Casey Little—Yo-Yo Queen* and *The Scream of the Hawk*. Nancy's writing has appeared in magazines in both Canada and the United States. She has acted in television commercials, training videos and documentaries. She is Managing Editor of the magazine *OUR HOMES (Windsor & Essex County)* and also works part-time as a library assistant.

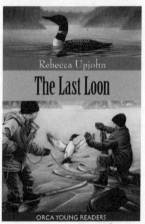

978-1-55469-292-7 $7.95 pb

Spending Christmas holidays in the wilderness with his ex-con Aunt Mag is not Evan's idea of a good time. What's worse is that everyone he meets—even his new friend Cedar—is making a big deal about a loon that is hanging around on the lake. Why should Evan care about a dumb bird? When he discovers that the loon will die without help, he realizes he does care, but rescuing the wild bird turns out to be a whole lot harder, and more dangerous, than he expected.

ORCA
YOUNG
READERS

Maureen Bush

Cursed!

ORCA YOUNG READERS

978-1-55469-286-6 $7.95 pb

Jane is terrified of the masks hanging in her grandmother's stairwell, and even more scared of the Spirit Man in her grandmother's bathroom. After a week of avoiding him during a summer visit, she finally summons the courage to face him, minutes before leaving for the trip home. But her moment of triumph marks the beginning of a year of trouble for Jane and her family, trouble only Jane (and the Spirit Man) can fix.